Unicorns are gentle peace-loving creatures, but they will fight fiercely to protect their young. They look like horses, but they are pure white. Truly magical creatures, they have a single twisted horn in the centre of their foreheads. The unicorns of Zavania have pastures on the lower slopes of the Mountains of Cloud, but each year the herd makes the hazardous journey through the terrible Enchanted Forest...

Look out for Maddie's further
adventures in Zavania. . .

Mermaid Wishes

Princess Wishes

Unicorn Wishes

Carol Barton

Illustrated by Charlotte Alder

Scholastic Children's Books,
Euston House, 24 Eversholt Street
London NW1 1DB, UK
A division of Scholastic Ltd
London ~ New York ~Toronto ~ Sydney ~ Auckland
Mexico City ~ New Delhi ~ Hong Kong

First published in the UK by Scholastic Ltd, 1999
This edition published by Scholastic Ltd, 2006

10 digit ISBN 0 439 95086 4
13 digit ISBN 978 0 439 95086 2

Printed and bound by Nørhaven Paperback A/S, Denmark

1 2 3 4 5 6 7 8 9 10

Papers used by Scholastic Children's Books are made from wood grown in
sustainable forests.

Contents

For Daniel, with love.

Chapter One

Sebastian

"Have you heard the latest?"

"No. What?"

"Maddie O'Neill's got a brace on her teeth!"

"As if she isn't ugly enough, with all those freckles."

"And that carroty hair!"

All day long the cruel taunts of her

class-mates rang in Maddie's ears. Not her friend Lucy of course. Lucy didn't join in with the others when they teased and bullied Maddie, she never did. On the other hand, neither was she able to do anything to stop them. Even when she tried, they simply laughed and called her Lucy Four-Eyes because she wore glasses.

Maddie had been in despair when her dentist said she had to wear the brace. "If you do," he said, "by the time you are sixteen you will have beautiful teeth."

"But I don't care about when I'm sixteen," Maddie wailed later to her mother. "I only care about now and what the others will say when I go to school and they see this awful thing."

"Maybe they won't say anything," Mum said hopefully, but Maddie knew they would.

When she got home from school she spent a whole hour in front of the mirror practising how she could smile or talk without showing her teeth, but it was almost impossible and the dreadful metal bars reminded Maddie of a monster she had once seen in a film. In the end, almost in tears, she made her way out of the house and into the garden.

The gardens of the row of houses where Maddie lived were very long and ran right down to a stream. There were a lot of trees at the bottom, ash trees, sycamores, and willows that dipped their branches right down into the water. Sometimes Maddie liked to make little paper boats which she would launch into the water then watch as they bobbed and dipped before disappearing downstream. But today she didn't feel like playing. Today, in spite of the fact that the sunlight was sparkling on the water, she still felt upset about what had happened at school.

She sat down on the bank and was about to take off her trainers and socks to dip her toes into the water, when a slight movement from beneath the curtain of willows caught her eye. With one hand on the bow of her laces she paused and peered into the cool green darkness. The movement came again and Maddie scrambled to her feet. Lifting one branch, she peered more closely into the gloom.

There was a boat moored there beneath the willows.

It was a long, flat boat partly covered with a piece of green canvas. Maddie stared at it in astonishment. It was very unusual to see a boat on this part of the stream. Further down some of the bigger houses had boats, and even landing stages, but that was after the stream joined the faster flowing river, not here in this quiet little backwater.

Cautiously she looked from left to right along the bank, wondering if the owner of the boat was anywhere around, but all was still, and save for the gentle lapping of the water against the side of the boat, very quiet.

Suddenly Maddie had an urge for a closer look. Steadying herself against the trunk of one of the willows she stepped into the boat. For one moment it rocked crazily. Thinking it might overturn and tip her into the water, Maddie hastily sat down.

There were cushions in the bottom of the boat, brightly coloured cushions with designs of birds; peacocks, pheasants and parrots. Reaching out her hand Maddie was just tracing the designs with one finger when she heard a sound, a noise like the cracking of a twig in the undergrowth on the bank.

She froze, lifting her head, listening.

It came again. Someone was coming along the bank of the stream. In a few seconds they would come into view under the branches of the willows.

Without even stopping to think, Maddie crouched down in the very bottom of the boat and pulled the green canvas cover over her head. Hopefully, whoever it was would soon pass by and she would be able to come out again.

Hardly daring to breathe she waited for what seemed a very long time, but there was no further sound, only the slight lurching of the boat.

She was just beginning to think that whoever it was had gone, or even that she might have been mistaken and that there hadn't been anyone there at all, when to her dismay, she realized that the boat was moving.

Softly, silently, it was sliding through the water.

At first, Maddie was too terrified to move.

Perhaps she was being kidnapped. She had heard stories of children who were kidnapped. Kidnappers were wicked people who held children captive then phoned their parents and demanded large sums of money, which usually had to be taken in a hold-all and left in a phone box.

Could this be what was happening to her? It seemed unlikely somehow, and besides it wouldn't do them any good because

Maddie's parents weren't even rich.

Maddie couldn't quite remember what kidnappers looked like. As she thought about it, she realized she wasn't entirely sure she'd even seen a photograph of a kidnapper.

Maybe if she lifted one corner of the green canvas she could have a look. Then perhaps, when the boat stopped, she might be able to escape and run back along the bank of the stream to her garden.

Slowly and very, very gently she lifted the edge of the canvas and peeped out.

At first, all she could see was a cloud of mist that seemed to be swirling around the boat, while drops of moisture dripped from the tips of the willow leaves into the stream. Moving slightly, she craned her neck and was just able to make out a figure at one end of the boat.

The figure was holding a long pole and Maddie watched through the tendrils of mist, as he dipped the pole deeply into the water and the boat slid forward again.

Maddie blinked, then briefly, as the mist dissolved, she could see more clearly. The figure holding the pole was that of a boy. A tall, slim boy probably a little older than Maddie herself. He was wearing a white shirt with huge sleeves, dark trousers that ended at his knees, and a long, black cloak.

His dark hair was like a close-fitting helmet. His skin was smooth like a peach and almost golden, while his eyes, as dark as his hair, were the shape of almonds, and seemed to lift very slightly at the corners beneath his straight black eyebrows. Slim brown hands held the pole as lovingly as if he played some musical instrument, while on the third finger of his right hand he wore a large diamond ring that flashed when it caught the light.

He certainly didn't look anything like Maddie expected a kidnapper to look.

In fact, if she was really truthful, he was the most beautiful person that she had ever seen.

Quite forgetting that she was supposed to be hiding, Maddie gaped at the boy while he, sensing he was being watched, turned and looked at her.

He seemed surprised, even shocked to find her there, which suggested he wasn't a kidnapper after all.

"Who are you?" he said, the almond-shaped eyes narrowing.

"Maddie," she said. "Maddie O'Neill."

"And what are you doing in my boat?"

"I only wanted to have a look," she said. "We don't often get boats in our part of the stream."

"I took a wrong turning," he said. "I had to get out on to the bank to get my bearings."

"So you aren't a kidnapper then?" she said.

"Of course not," he replied indignantly. "Do I look like a kidnapper?"

Maddie shook her head. She didn't want to admit that she had no idea what a kidnapper looked like.

"Can you take me home?" she said after a moment, when the boat still seemed to be gliding forward at quite an alarming pace.

"Not right at this moment I can't," said the boy. "I'm on my way to see my master to find out the details of my next assignment, and I'm late as it is."

"Oh dear," said Maddie. "What am I going to do?"

"You could come with me if you like," said the boy.

"I'm not sure that I should." Maddie crawled right out from under the canvas. "How far are you going?"

"I have to go to the castle first but after that I shall be on my way. Come with me if you want. I shall be glad of your company."

"Will you?" Maddie stared at him in

amazement. He had a strange, lilting sort of voice which sounded almost as if he was singing instead of talking.

"Of course," said the boy. "It gets very lonely sometimes you know, especially when the job takes you far away."

"Well yes," Maddie agreed. "I suppose it would." She paused, watching him as he arched his neck and let the pole slide through his fingers. His neck was long and curved like a swan's. "But – er – where exactly would we be going?" she asked.

"I told you, I won't know until after I've been to the castle. My master has his rooms there in the East Tower, he will explain the details."

"I'm not allowed to stay out too long," said Maddie.

"Don't worry about that," said the boy with a cool smile. "You'll be back at the exact time you should be."

"How do you know that if you don't know where we are going?" asked Maddie.

"You just have to trust me," said the boy.

"I don't know about that," said Maddie uneasily. Much as she wanted to go with him to this castle, wherever it was, she knew she shouldn't. Her mother had warned her against going anywhere with strangers, and after all, that was what this boy was. "I really think," she said at last, "that I'd better go home now."

The boy, however, didn't seem to be listening to her. Instead he was peering ahead through the mist, bending forward slightly as the boat slid noiselessly under the last of the willows.

Quite suddenly there was no more mist, only sunlight, bright sunlight that danced and sparkled on the water, and the stream had become a river, wider and faster-flowing.

In astonishment Maddie gazed around her. There was no sign of the big houses that she knew were further downstream. Instead, on either side were fields of lush green grass filled with wild flowers; scarlet poppies, daisies, and deep blue cornflowers.

In the distance purple mountains soared into the endless blue of the sky, their tops white with snow. Around the boat fish jumped in the water while brightly painted butterflies chased one another, and the sweet notes of a songbird filled the air.

"Oh," Maddie gasped. "Where are we?"

"What do you mean?" The boy turned to look at her leaning against the pole as the current bore the boat along. "Haven't you been here before?"

"Well, I've been downstream once, in my uncle's rowing boat," she said, "but I don't remember it being like this. What is this place?"

"This is Zavania," said the boy.

"Oh," said Maddie again, then she hesitated. Really she very much wanted to go with him. "If I came with you, would you get me back in time for tea?" she asked.

"Of course." The boy nodded.

"In that case," said Maddie slowly, "I think I will."

"Good," said the boy. "You can help me."

"If I'm going to help you," said Maddie, "I think I should know your name. After all, I've told you mine."

"So you have," said the boy. "You're Maddie. And I," he gave a mysterious smile, "am Sebastian."

Chapter Two

The Raven

"Sebastian what?" asked Maddie curiously.

"Just Sebastian," said the boy, with a shrug.

"Don't you have another name?" Maddie demanded.

"No," he replied. "Zak named me Sebastian."

"Who is Zak?"

"You ask a lot of questions," said Sebastian. "Zak belongs to the WishMaster. You will meet them both when we reach the royal castle."

Maddie stared at him in astonishment. "Whatever is a WishMaster?" she asked.

"The chief granter of wishes," replied the boy, straightening up and peering down the river. While they had been talking they had travelled quite a distance, and the fields and banks of the river seemed to be slipping by at a quite alarming rate.

"I don't know what you mean," said Maddie.

"It's quite simple," Sebastian replied. "Someone makes a wish. My master, Zenith, decides whether or not it's important enough to be an Official Wish. If it is, he has to set about granting it. And that's what I'm training to do – the granting of wishes. That's where we're going now," he added when Maddie continued to stare at him, "to see the WishMaster, so that he can tell me what my next assignment is."

"But how exciting," said Maddie. "What sort of things do people wish for?"

"Oh, all sorts of things," said Sebastian.

"But what things?" demanded Maddie. She was burning with curiosity by now.

"Well," the boy lifted his head as if considering, "take last week for instance. Zenith sent me to the royal gardens because the Princess Lyra had made a wish. I discovered the wish was that she wanted to ride on the back of a black swan."

"And were you able to grant that?" asked Maddie in amazement.

"No," replied Sebastian. "When I told

Zenith what the wish was he said it wasn't important enough to be an Official Wish even though it had been the princess who had made it."

"So what did she say?" asked Maddie curiously.

"She didn't like it." Sebastian said grimly. "But there you are, Zenith's decision is final."

"So tell me about a wish you *have* granted," said Maddie.

"I've just done one now as it happens," said Sebastian casually. "That's where I was coming from when you found my boat. Sometimes I have to travel very long distances but this one wasn't too far away. I had to go to a place called Dragon's Rock, because one of the dragons who lives there couldn't breathe fire. And let's face it, a dragon who can't breathe fire isn't much use to anyone, is it?"

"No, I suppose not," said Maddie faintly. "But I didn't think there were such things as dragons," she added.

"You'd better not let the dragons in the royal mews hear you say that," said Sebastian darkly. "They can get very hot-tempered if anyone upsets them."

"So what was this dragon's wish?"

"That he could breathe fire like any normal dragon," Sebastian replied.

"And were you able to grant that?" asked Maddie in awe.

"Yes, in the end I did," said Sebastian.

"What do you mean, in the end?"

"Well, Zenith allows me two magic spells to help me with each wish," he explained. "And I had a bit of trouble getting the words of one of the spells just right. I'm still learning, you see."

"So how do you make these spells work?" asked Maddie. "Do you wave a magic wand?"

"No, I have to say the magic words and I use this." Sebastian flicked back his cloak and pointed to the ring on his finger with its large stone. "Zenith changes the ring for each set of spells," he went on. "As you can see, this time it was a diamond. Once before it was an amethyst. Another time it might be a ruby and so on, but whatever it is, it conducts the magic to perform the spells."

"You say you have two spells for each wish?" asked Maddie, and when Sebastian nodded she went on, "So if these spells are magic couldn't you just use one, say to get you to wherever it is you have to go, and the other to grant the wish?"

"It isn't that simple," replied Sebastian – a little huffily, Maddie thought. "I have to prove to Zenith that I can use the spells wisely. Besides, what would I do if I found myself in a dangerous situation after the wish had been granted and I'd used both my spells? How do you think I would get back?"

"Oh," said Maddie, "I see what you mean."

"When I have granted many Official Wishes," the boy went on, "I earn my Golden Spurs."

"Oh," said Maddie again. "What are they?"

"They are to prove that I am no longer an apprentice – that I too have become a fully-fledged WishMaster," proclaimed Sebastian, proudly drawing himself up to his full height.

Maddie was speechless at this and simply clasped her hands together in admiration.

Sebastian seemed to glow for a moment, then suddenly his head shot up. "Oh no!" he exclaimed.

"What is it?" said Maddie, alarmed by the note of fear in his voice.

"Harromin," said Sebastian. "He won't let us pass."

Maddie looked around and was amazed to find that while Sebastian had been telling her about his job the fields of wild flowers that they had been passing through had disappeared, and given way to harsh rocks and cliffs that towered on either side of them.

"Who is Harromin?" she whispered, clutching on to either side of the boat in sudden fear.

"He's there," said Sebastian in a low voice. "There, on that rock."

Slowly, fearfully, Maddie followed his gaze, and there on a flat rock that jutted out over the water she saw what appeared to be the figure of a huge, fat toad.

But he was no ordinary toad. He was a muddy, orangey colour and his skin was speckled with purplish spots. He also had hair, a thick tuft of wiry black hair that grew between his round, unblinking eyes. And he had a tail, which Maddie thought was very strange for a toad. It was a long, pointed tail that swished backwards and forwards on the rock with a dry, rasping sound.

Sebastian had dug the pole into the bed of the river and as the boat bobbed precariously on the water he eyed the fat toad warily.

"We want to pass, Harromin," he said firmly at last.

"Who's that with you?" said the toad in a flat, dull voice.

Maddie stared at him in astonishment. Whoever had heard of a toad who talked!

"Her name is Maddie," said Sebastian.

The toad suddenly spat at them.

"Oh, how rude," gasped Maddie, recoiling.

"I want her hair," snapped the toad.

"Whatever does he mean?" Maddie frowned.

"You can't have her hair, Harromin," said Sebastian calmly. "It belongs to her."

"I like it," said the toad. "It's better than mine. I want it. If you don't let me have it, I won't let you pass."

"Don't be silly, Harromin," said Sebastian. "You can't have Maddie's hair, and you have to let us pass. I have a job to do for Zenith. He won't be very pleased with you if you don't let us pass through the gorge."

The toad swished his tail angrily. "Zenith doesn't scare me." He spat again. "If you try to pass, I'll sink your boat."

"Oh, Sebastian," gasped Maddie. "What can we do? I don't want to give him my hair." Most of the time Maddie hated her hair and the way it sprang into crisp curls like corkscrews, but on the other hand she wasn't sure that she wanted to part with it either. She was afraid she would look even sillier if she was bald.

"Looks like we may have to turn back and wait until after he's gone," murmured Sebastian in a low voice so that the toad wouldn't hear him. "He means what he says – he really would sink the boat if that's what he had made up his mind to do."

"Oh dear," said Maddie. "What a beastly toad he is. Isn't there anything we can do?" She looked round in desperation at the smooth cliff face that towered on either side of them, at the squat hump of the evil toad basking in the heat on his rock, at the endless blue of the sky and the deep green of the water around the boat.

"I suppose I could try a spell," said Sebastian. He sounded a little dubious.

Maddie stared at him. "Oh yes!" she cried, then when still he seemed to hesitate and the toad swished his tail again, she said, "Well, go on then, do one – now!"

"I don't think it'll work, not without Zenith's approval," he went on in the same low tones.

"Well, try it anyway," gasped Maddie desperately. "We've got to do something!"

Sebastian cleared his throat and rather hesitantly began chanting:

"Zaspa, Zespa, Zen,
Zespa, Zaspa, Zon,
Zessapazee and Zessapazoo. . ."

He trailed off. "Oh, what's next?" he muttered. "I can't remember. . ."

Harromin gave a shriek of mirth and prepared to launch himself at the boat, then quite suddenly everything went dark as the sun was blotted out.

Maddie gave a little cry, Sebastian turned sharply and the boat lurched as a black shape descended on them, rushing towards them through the air at a terrifying speed.

The fat toad's eyes seemed to bulge right out of his head as the shape, which Maddie could now see was a large black bird, swooped and dived, then hovered above, its claws extended, its sharp beak ready to peck.

With a strangled gulp the toad was gone, over the side of the rock, falling into

the water with an enormous plop.

For a moment Maddie was speechless as she looked up again at the huge black bird. Then, to her horror, Sebastian seemed to sway, and for one terrible moment she thought he too was going to topple over into the water. It seemed they had got rid of one danger only to have it replaced by another.

In that instant Maddie knew she had to do something.

Standing up in the boat she began waving her arms. "Go away, you horrible bird!" she cried. "Leave us alone. Go on, shoo! Shoo!"

"Maddie! Maddie!"

She turned as she realized that Sebastian was calling her. "Don't worry!" she yelled back. "I'll make him go away." She carried on flapping her arms while the boat rocked and tilted crazily and the large black bird perched calmly on the top of the pole and eyed her up and down.

"It's all right, Maddie," cried Sebastian. "Really it is. This is the raven."

"Well, I can see that," said Maddie. "But he needn't think *he*'s going to scare us as well, because he isn't. That fat old toad was bad enough and I'm not having any more of it." With her hands on her hips she stared crossly at Sebastian and the raven.

"No, Maddie," said Sebastian. "You don't understand. This is Zak. He belongs to my master, Zenith. . ."

"So what's he doing trying to frighten us?" demanded Maddie, her face red now, nearly as red as her curls, which were bobbing up and down.

"He isn't," said Sebastian, and to add to

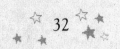

Maddie's anger she saw that he was trying not to laugh.

"So what was he doing then for goodness sake, flapping around like that, sticking out his claws and pointing his beak?" she demanded, glaring at the raven.

"He was rescuing us," said Sebastian.

"What do you mean, rescuing us? He nearly made you fall into the water. I don't call that rescuing us."

"He's frightened Harromin away," Sebastian pointed out. "Harromin has always been afraid of Zak. He won't try to stop us from passing him now."

"Won't he?" Dubiously, Maddie peered over the side of the boat in the general direction in which the toad had disappeared.

For the moment all she could see was an ever-widening series of ripples as they spread out further and further across the river, then she gave a little shriek and pointed. "Look," she cried, "there he is!"

Above the surface of the water two unblinking eyes could be seen, watching them. "He's still there," she said.

"So he may be," said Sebastian grimly. "But he won't dare to stop us now, not with Zak here." As he spoke the raven stood up on the end of the pole and flapped his huge black wings, just once, but it was enough for Harromin, who rapidly disappeared under the water once more.

Maddie looked at the raven and suddenly felt a bit ashamed of herself for having misjudged him so badly. "I'm sorry," she said gruffly. "But I didn't know who you were."

"That's OK," said the raven. "I tend to forget these claws and this beak frighten folks. I'm so used to them, you see." He turned his head and looked up into Sebastian's face. "So who's your friend?" he asked.

"This is Maddie," said Sebastian. "She's coming with me on the next assignment."

"Really?" said Zak. "Any special reason?"

"Not particularly," Sebastian shrugged. "I just thought it might be fun to have her along." To Maddie's amazement she saw a slow flush spread over Sebastian's smooth face.

"Oh boy!" said Zak. "That won't be good enough for Zenith. You know that." He turned his head and looked at Maddie. "Anything you are really good at?"

"I don't think so," said Maddie. "Not especially."

"That won't do," squawked the raven. "Think. What are you best at at school?"

"Um . . . well, I like painting. . ."

"Very nice, I'm sure, but not a lot of use on an assignment. . ."

"And I like poetry and drama. . . I got the lead in the school play at the end of term. . ."

"Now that could be useful," said Zak thoughtfully. "Good at learning lines, are you?"

Maddie nodded. "Oh yes, I learnt all my lines in two evenings."

The raven flapped his wings again, "Like I say," he said, "that could be useful. But if we don't get a move on, we'll all be out of a job. Zenith's in quite a mood today, I warn you. He sent me to hurry you up, Sebastian."

"Oh dear," said Sebastian pulling the pole from the water again. "We'd best hurry then. Do you know what the job is, Zak?"

"Sort of," said Zak. "It's to do with the princess. There's chaos at the castle."

"Oh no, not again," sighed Sebastian. "What has she wished for this time, the moon?"

"It isn't her that's actually made the wish," Zak replied. "It's a little unicorn."

"Oh?" said Sebastian. "So what's that got to do with the princess?"

"Well, it appears that unbeknownst to anyone, she's been keeping the little chap as a pet," said Zak.

"But it's against the law in Zavania to keep unicorns in captivity," said Sebastian indignantly. "The king says all unicorns must be allowed to run free."

"Well, I can assure you, the princess obviously doesn't think that sort of thing applies to her. She reckons," Zak went on, "that because she found this little one wandering on the edge of the forest, he now belongs to her."

"And what does the king have to say about that?" asked Sebastian.

"He doesn't know yet," Zak replied. "He and the queen are still away on their state visit, but sparks will fly when they return, you can be sure of that."

"I still don't understand," said Sebastian. "What's the wish?"

"I don't know," said Zak, spreading his wings and flying alongside them through the gorge. "You'll just have to wait until you see Zenith, then you can ask him yourself."

Chapter Three

The Unicorn's Wish

Maddie opened her mouth to say that there were no such things as unicorns and certainly not unicorns who went around making wishes, but she thought better of it and closed her mouth again. It seemed that in this strange land many things were possible, and if you could have dragons, and toads who talked, it was probably perfectly reasonable to have baby unicorns making wishes.

They were now moving quite rapidly down river, borne along by the current while Sebastian held the pole and the raven, Zak, perched on the top. They were through the cliffs and rocks of the gorge and now, on either side, were wide fields of tall grasses and rich, waving corn. In the distance could be seen thick forests of dark green fir trees. Just visible above the tops of the trees Maddie could see a building with white towers, and flags that fluttered in the wind from its many pointed turrets.

"Is that the castle?" she asked, craning her neck for a better look.

"Yes." Sebastian half-turned in the boat. "That's where I live."

"It looks beautiful," said Maddie, "and

very, very grand." She fell silent thinking of her own house by the river, which was little more than a cottage and really quite small.

"Do you live with your parents?" she asked after a while, then she jumped as Zak suddenly spread his wings and flapped them a couple of times. Maddie eyed him warily. She still wasn't quite sure about this huge, black bird with its sharp beak and claws. She was far more interested in Sebastian. But it was the raven who answered her question.

"He doesn't have any parents," he said.

"Oh," said Maddie glancing quickly at Sebastian who had turned away again and was staring ahead as if he was concentrating on where he was going.

He looked a lonely figure as he stood aloof at the end of the boat.

"It was me who found him, you know," said Zak.

"Really?" Maddie began to feel a bit uncomfortable that they were talking like this about Sebastian, as if he wasn't there. Zak, however, didn't seem to have any such worries.

"Little scrap of a thing he was," he said. "He was left on the steps of the East Tower in a basket."

"In a basket?" said Maddie faintly, with a quick glance at the back of Sebastian's head. She was fascinated now, in spite of herself.

"Yep," cackled the raven with a throaty chuckle. "I picked up the basket in my beak and took it up the stairs to Zenith's room."

"The WishMaster?" breathed Maddie. She could tell that Sebastian was listening now, but it was almost as if he'd heard the story so many times before that he didn't appear to be too bothered by it.

"That's him," said Zak. "He wasn't there at the time, as it happened, he'd gone out on an assignment. There'd been some trouble over at the Ice Palace – some things never change – a skirmish between the king's soldiers and the Ice Army if I remember rightly. . ."

"But what did you do?" interrupted Maddie. "With the baby, I mean . . . with Sebastian. . .?" She wasn't in the slightest bit interested in all this talk of ice and soldiers but she was desperate to know what had happened to Sebastian.

"Oh, I left him with Thirza," Zak replied in an off-hand sort of way. "You wouldn't believe the fuss she made over him – all that cooing and aahing—"

"Who is Thirza?" asked Maddie in bewilderment. She was getting thoroughly confused now with all these strange-sounding names.

"She takes care of Zenith – a sort of housekeeper I suppose – you'll meet her in a bit."

"Oh," said Maddie. "Oh, I see." She paused, then after a moment she said, "So what did Zenith – the WishMaster, I mean," she hastily corrected herself after another glance at the back of Sebastian's head – "what did he say when he came home?"

Zak gave another cackle. "He wasn't too happy at first, I can tell you. Said the turret room was no place for a baby and that he had to go."

"Oh dear," said Maddie, wondering what on earth Sebastian was thinking, "so what happened?"

"Thirza begged Zenith to let the baby stay. She said she would care for him herself, just as if he was her own, and that she wouldn't let him get in the way of Zenith's work, or be a bother to him in any way."

"So what happened then?" Maddie clasped her hands together. She was vaguely aware that while they had been talking, Sebastian had brought the boat into a sort of landing stage, but for the moment she was too enthralled by the story the raven was telling.

"Well, he let him stay in the end," Zak went on. "Course he did. Old Zenith's bark is far worse than his bite, you know. Thirza cares for him, and Zenith teaches him the things he needs to know—"

"And you protect him," said Maddie.

"What?" squawked Zak.

"You protect him from danger," she said. "Like you did just now from Harromin."

"Oh, Harromin," said Zak contemptuously with another flap of his wings. Then gruffly, he admitted, "Well yes, I suppose I do look out for Sebastian. Always have, I guess. But I keep telling him, he's got to stand on his own two feet. I might not always be around to look out for him. . ."

"I know that, Zak," said Sebastian unexpectedly. "Here, make yourself useful and take this rope."

Muttering and squawking to himself the raven took the rope in his beak and flew on to the landing stage where, very carefully, he threaded the end through a large metal ring, holding it firmly while Sebastian sprang ashore.

After tying the boat up securely

Sebastian swirled the black cloak around him, turned and held out his hand. Maddie stood up and took his hand and while he steadied her, she stepped ashore. With Zak flying alongside they walked along the narrow landing-stage.

"These are the royal gardens," said Sebastian a few moments later as they walked through pathways of crazy-paving, between strongly-scented flowering bushes of every colour that Maddie could think of. "The river took us directly into the grounds. If we'd come the other way we would have had to ask the castle guards to raise the portcullis so that we could cross the drawbridge."

"Always a tedious business," said Zak. "All that creaking and groaning and then they want to know so much before they let you in. Last time they pretended they didn't know who we were, didn't they Sebastian? Silly lot," he added when Sebastian nodded, "too full of their own importance if you ask me."

They passed through an archway of cream, trumpet-shaped flowers that cascaded over wooden rafters to the ground, then found themselves on smooth velvet lawns surrounded by a high brick wall. White statues were set into little niches in the red brickwork and what seemed like hundreds of fountains sent jets of cool water high into the air.

"The water's pink!" said Maddie in amazement, as she stopped for a moment to stare.

"Yes," Sebastian agreed, then he added, "and it's raspberry flavoured."

"Raspberry?" Maddie stared at the water again, wondering if she dared to stop and taste it to see for herself if what Sebastian said was true.

"The princess had the fountains all changed one year for her birthday," muttered Zak. "Silly child. It's about time someone said No to her for once. She gets far too much of her own way if you ask me. Mind you, she's not going to like this wish. . . ."

Sebastian stopped dead and stared at Zak. "You know what the wish is, don't you?" he said accusingly.

"Might do," mumbled Zak, as if he feared he'd said too much.

"So what is it?" demanded Sebastian.

"Perhaps you'd better go and see Zenith first," said Zak uneasily.

"No," said Sebastian. "If you're not going to tell me, I'll go and see this unicorn myself. If I'm to be the one who's going to grant this wish I think I should know what it is, especially when everyone else seems to know already."

With another swirl of his cloak Sebastian turned on his heel and began striding off down another pathway.

"Oh, I say, wait a minute," croaked Zak. "Don't go off in a huff."

But it was too late, for without so much as a backward glance, Sebastian was halfway down the path. With a great sigh Zak swooped after him. Maddie hesitated for a moment, but she was terrified that she might be left behind in the garden. It might seem pleasant with its raspberry-flavoured fountains and wonderfully-scented flowers but it was, after all, pretty weird. She took to her heels and sped after the striding figure of Sebastian, and the raven who was flapping alongside him, tutting and squawking.

"Zenith won't like this," fussed Zak as Maddie caught them up. "You know how he likes to tell you about the assignments himself. Sebastian, please be reasonable. . ."

But Sebastian wasn't listening, and Maddie was forced to run even faster just to keep up with him as he swept through a doorway. They passed under yet another archway, this time built of stone instead of flowers, and into a courtyard that reminded Maddie of the riding school where her friend Lucy went for lessons.

"This is the royal mews," said Zak for Maddie's benefit. "All the king's animals are kept here."

There were stalls all round the outside of the courtyard, and inside them the

horses were dozing gently in the sunshine, nodding their heads over the stable doors. One or two opened their eyes at the sudden intrusion and whickered softly, hoping, no doubt, for some tasty titbit, but Sebastian ignored them, turning instead to Zak. "Right, where is he?" he demanded.

"I'm not really sure. . ." Zak began to bluster.

"Then I'll find him myself." Sebastian strode on through the yard looking from left to right as he went.

"Oh cripes!" muttered Zak. Then looking at Maddie, he said, "Come on, I suppose we'd better go with him. There'll be no stopping him now."

Maddie hurried after the raven and they found themselves in a smaller yard at the rear of the stables. Sebastian was standing in the centre, hands on his hips as he stared around him.

"He's in there," croaked Zak, nodding towards a small building in one corner of the yard. "Princess Lyra's play house."

The building was like a little castle with four turrets, one at each corner and all joined by battlements. Sebastian strode towards it and turned the handle on the studded wooden door. He pushed it open, and followed by Maddie and the still grumbling raven, went inside.

It was cool and dim, the walls were whitewashed and there were fresh, sweet-smelling rushes on the floor.

It took a little while for Maddie's eyes to become accustomed to the dimness. Then at the far end of the room she saw that a single lamp burned above a sort of platform. On the platform, in the middle of a bed of straw, was a little animal.

But it was an animal the likes of which Maddie had only seen in picture books. It was pure white, with the appearance of a horse, but in the centre of its forehead was one single twisted horn.

Sebastian slowly approached the platform. "Hello," he said. "I'm Sebastian."

It came as no great surprise to Maddie when the little unicorn answered. She was beginning to expect anything now in this strange land.

"Hello, Sebastian." The little unicorn had a very soft, gentle voice and big, sad eyes.

"Zak tells me you've made a wish," Sebastian went on.

The little unicorn nodded.

"Are you going to tell me what it is?" asked Sebastian gently, and when the little unicorn didn't reply he went on, "I think you should, because I'm the one who will be granting your wish."

The little unicorn turned his head and looked at Maddie, as if he wondered who she was and what she was doing in his stable.

"This is Maddie," said Sebastian. "She's going to help me. So will you tell me now what it is?"

The little unicorn made a noise that sounded like a great sigh. "I want to go home," he said at last.

"Home?" said Sebastian. "But isn't this your home now?"

"No," said the little unicorn. "Not really." He shook his head and to her dismay Maddie saw a large tear roll down his face. It trembled for a moment on the tip of his velvety nose before plopping on to the straw. "I want to go back to my herd and see my mother again," he said at last.

Chapter Four

The East Tower

Maddie found there was a huge lump in her throat and she had to swallow furiously, afraid that she was going to cry. But at that very moment a dark shadow fell across them, blotting out the sunlight that streamed through the open door.

Maddie looked up and blinked but all she could see was the dark outline of someone standing in the doorway.

Zak gave a single squawk and Sebastian, who had sunk to his knees beside the little unicorn, scrambled quickly to his feet.

"Your Highness," he said, gathering his cloak around him and bowing deeply.

Startled, Maddie screwed up her eyes for a better look. By now the figure had moved round away from the bright sunlight and Maddie could see it was a girl. She was probably a little older than Maddie, tall, with very pale skin, large blue eyes and thick straight hair that fell to her waist like a curtain and was the same colour as the ripe corn in the fields.

"What are you doing here?" the girl demanded in a haughty voice. "And who is she?" She glared at Maddie, and Zak gave a cackle of laughter. "Be quiet," she said to the raven, "or I'll have you shot and hung out in the fields to scare the crows."

Zak flapped his wings indignantly but stayed silent, while Maddie looked at him in alarm. Surely this girl couldn't do that to poor Zak? Before she had a chance to protest however, Sebastian spoke again.

"This is Maddie," he said.

"But *who* is she exactly?" The girl eyed Maddie up and down, seeming to take in every detail of her appearance, from her red curls to the checked shirt and blue jeans she was wearing. She had an expression on her face that suggested she had just caught a whiff of an extremely unpleasant smell.

"She's a friend," said Sebastian simply. "She's from the Other Place."

"Well, I don't like her," said the girl.

"She's got bad teeth."

"I haven't got bad teeth!" retorted Maddie.

"Then what's that awful contraption in your mouth?" sneered the girl.

Zak gave a muffled squawk and the little unicorn whickered softly as if he sensed the tension in the air and dreaded what might follow.

"It's a brace," said Maddie, holding on to her temper with difficulty. "It's to straighten my teeth."

"So why do they need straightening?" said the girl, with a spiteful little smile.

"Because they are crooked," said Maddie.

"Just what I said: *bad*," said the girl, with a shrug. Turning away she walked across to the little unicorn and crouching down beside him, began to stroke his nose.

Maddie would have flown after her, said more, set the matter right, but Sebastian placed a restraining hand on her arm. "Best to leave it," he said softly in her ear.

"But. . ." she began.

"No." He shook his head, then leaving her to cool down he too went across to the little unicorn.

"You know he has made a wish, don't you?" he said to the princess.

"I heard a silly rumour," she said coolly, without looking up.

"So you know what the wish is?" asked Sebastian. When the girl didn't reply he went on, "He wants to go back to his mother."

"That's ridiculous," said the girl. Still she didn't look up, continuing instead to stroke the little unicorn's pure white coat. "Of course he doesn't. He's mine, I found him and he will stay here with me."

"But he's already made the wish," said Sebastian.

"Then I shall make another wish." The girl stood up and tossed back her golden hair. "My wish will be that he stays here with me."

"But you know the rules," said Sebastian. "If Zenith has already pronounced that this is an Official Wish. . ."

"What do I care for any stupid rules?" cried the girl. "I am the Princess Lyra – I can make my own rules." With her blue eyes flashing she stared defiantly at Sebastian.

"Don't you think a word with Zenith might settle this?" said Zak suddenly from above them on the beam in the roof where he had perched, well out of the princess's way.

"I told you once to shut up, you silly bird," said Princess Lyra. "This is all your fault anyway. If you hadn't gone poking that beak in where it isn't wanted none of this would have happened. My unicorn was perfectly happy until you started interfering."

"But isn't it against the law to keep a unicorn as a pet?" asked Maddie.

"What do you know about it?" The princess rounded on Maddie. "It's nothing to do with you. Besides, silly laws don't apply to me."

It was Sebastian who answered. "Zenith is the WishMaster," he said firmly. "And his word is law concerning any wishes that are made."

The little unicorn nodded but the Princess Lyra turned on her heel. "I shall speak to the Lord Chamberlain," she retorted and marched off, away through the royal mews.

"Come on, Maddie," said Sebastian. Then turning to the little unicorn he added, "We'll be back soon."

"What will the Lord Chamberlain do?"

gasped Maddie as she ran beside Sebastian.

"Well, he won't tangle with Zenith, that's for sure," chuckled Zak, who'd flown down to join them as soon as the princess had gone. "It's more than his job's worth. I told you you should have gone to see Zenith first, didn't I?" he said with a sly, sidelong glance at Sebastian.

"I know," snapped Sebastian. "You were right, but then you usually are, Zak. Just don't keep on about it, all right?"

The castle was quite magnificent at close quarters, with high, arched windows set with thousands of tiny panes of glass that glittered and twinkled in the sunlight. The white walls were dazzling, while the flags and pennants that fluttered from the turrets were of red, blue, green and yellow. An inner moat of turquoise water surrounded the castle and they crossed this by means of a little rustic footbridge.

Maddie paused for a moment in the middle of the bridge and gazed down into the crystal clear waters, where rainbow-coloured fish played amongst tiger-lilies and huge dragonflies hovered before darting away, their wings sparkling like gossamer.

She would have liked to linger, for she'd never seen fish such as these or dragonflies of such a size, but Sebastian called out from the far side of the bridge where he had stopped and was waiting for her.

"Hurry, Maddie," he said. "I'll be in real trouble with the WishMaster if I don't get there soon. I have to give him a full report on the dragon's wish and how I used the spells."

"Coming." Reluctantly Maddie dragged

herself away and hurried after Sebastian and Zak.

Together they skirted the walls of the great castle and eventually they came to one tower that seemed a little different from all the others. It was white, as the others were, but there were many signs and symbols carved into the smooth stonework: symbols depicting the sun, the moon and the stars; others of strange mythical animals: dragons, griffins, horses with wings and centaurs – half-horse and half-man.

Maddie knew about these creatures because her teacher had started a project at school and they had made a huge collage that had taken up one entire wall in Class Four's room. Maddie wondered what they would say when she told them about all she had seen since coming to Zavania.

Sebastian had opened a door at the base of the tower and was beckoning her inside. Zak had gone ahead, swooping past them up a staircase that twisted up and up, round and round, with hundreds of steep, stone steps.

Maddie was just wondering if the staircase would ever come to an end when it suddenly opened out into a wide room.

The room was very clean, the floor strewn with fresh rushes, the walls hung with tapestries of parrots and peacocks woven in bright, jewel-coloured wool, just like those on the cushions in Sebastian's boat.

A table which ran the entire length of the room had been set for a meal. There was a huge bowl of fresh fruit in the centre, and at one end a board with several oddly-shaped loaves of bread. There was a raised dais at one end of the room with wooden steps leading down to the floor.

Maddie looked up and saw that someone was standing there watching them. At first she thought it was a child, then with a little start, she realized it was a woman, a tiny woman, much smaller even than Maddie herself, with nut-brown skin wrinkled like a walnut shell, her hair plaited around her head and eyes like tiny black currants.

"Who is this?" The woman's voice was high-pitched, shrill, almost like the notes of a bell.

"This is Maddie," said Sebastian patiently. Maddie thought he must be getting fed up telling everyone who she was. "She's going to help me," he added.

"Does Zenith know about this?" The woman stared down at them, her hands on her hips. Zak had flown up to the platform and was perched on her shoulder.

"Not yet, Thirza," replied Sebastian. "I'm hoping he won't mind."

So this was Thirza, thought Maddie. The woman who had looked after Sebastian ever since Zak had found him on the steps when he was a baby.

"Is he in a good mood?" Maddie detected an anxious note in Sebastian's voice.

"Well, he was," said Thirza with a sniff. "But that was before you were late. He's been stomping about up there for the last hour or so."

Zak gave a cackle of laughter and Sebastian glanced first up at the ceiling, then towards yet more steps that curved upwards in one corner of the room.

"I suppose we'd better go up," he said reluctantly. "Come on, Maddie."

"Not so fast," snapped Thirza, her black eyes glittering like tiny pieces of coal. "You go up, Sebastian. Let the girl stay with me."

Maddie's heart sank. She didn't want to stay with anyone, she wanted to go with Sebastian. She felt safe with him. She looked quickly at him, saw him hesitate, thought he was about to disregard Thirza, when suddenly there came a thunderous knocking sound on the ceiling and they all froze.

"Where is he? Wretched boy!" The booming voice was nearly as loud as the knocking. "If he isn't here in two minutes we'll see how he likes life as a toad."

Sebastian moved so fast Maddie hardly saw him go, across the room, and up the staircase that curved away out of sight.

"I told him to hurry," cackled Zak as he left Thirza's shoulder and flew down, settling on the back of a chair. Thirza herself clumped down the wooden steps that led from the dais to the floor.

"So where do you come from?" She eyed Maddie up and down, but not in an unkind way as Princess Lyra had done. "You can't be one of the Little People, you are too big."

Zak laughed again. "You're right there, Thirza," he said. "She's from the Other Place."

"Oh, she is, is she!" exclaimed Thirza darkly. "Well, let's hope there won't be any trouble. Seems to me, whenever there's any dealings with the Other Place, there's trouble."

"I won't cause any trouble, I promise," said Maddie. "All I'm going to do is help Sebastian."

"Hmm," said Thirza. Then turning to

Zak, she said, "has the Princess Lyra seen her yet?"

"Oh yes." Zak sounded quite gleeful. "You should have seen her face."

"That's what I mean by trouble," said Thirza.

"We're only going to take the little unicorn back to his mother," protested Maddie.

"How do you know about that?" snapped Thirza. Then rounding on Zak, she said, "I suppose you told them. It's about time you learned to keep your beak shut – it'll get you in a lot of trouble one day. You mark my words. You know Zenith is the one to tell Sebastian what his tasks are to be."

"Yeah, yeah, I know," muttered Zak, allowing his head to sink right down between his hunched wings.

"How did you meet Sebastian?" Thirza

rounded on Maddie now.

"Oh." Maddie jumped. "I saw his boat in the stream at the bottom of my garden," she said hastily. "It was empty," she went on, when Thirza remained silent as if awaiting more explanation, "and I climbed inside. I heard somebody coming and I hid. The next thing I knew the boat was moving . . . and . . . and Sebastian asked me if I'd like to go with him and help him to grant wishes."

"It's OK," said Zak. "She's quite suitable."

"Hmm," said Thirza, "we shall see. Well, now that you're here, you'd better have something to eat. I'll set another place at the table."

"That's awfully kind of you," said Maddie. "Thank you very much."

The little woman began bustling about

74

with wooden plates and goblets. Maddie glanced at Zak, a little uncertain what she should do next, and was surprised when the raven closed one eye in a huge wink.

"So where's this house of yours with the stream at the bottom of the garden?" said Thirza a moment later, as she poured thick, strawberry-coloured liquid from a large jug into the goblets.

"Oh, it's not far from Salisbury," said Maddie.

"And who do you live there with?" It seemed Thirza needed to know everything there was to know about Sebastian's new friend.

"Just my mum and my dad," said Maddie. "And Whisker, my cat."

"So is your father a landowner?" Thirza's eyes narrowed so much they almost disappeared.

"Well, yes." Maddie frowned, thinking of their garden where Dad grew his vegetables. "I suppose he is. He's also a postman," she added quickly. "And Mum works in an old people's home. She's a care assistant. . ." She broke off in mid-sentence as there came a sudden noise from the corner of the room and Sebastian appeared on the staircase once more.

"Come on Maddie," he said, beckoning furiously. "The WishMaster wants to meet you."

"Oh dear." Maddie wiped the palms of her hands down the side of her jeans.

"Best of luck," croaked Zak. "I'll keep my feathers crossed that he's in a good mood. If he's going to turn Sebastian into a toad you could well find yourself becoming a tadpole, or if he's in a really generous mood, maybe a moth."

Chapter Five

The WishMaster

Maddie had seen pictures of wizards, magicians and sorcerers, and if she remembered correctly, most seemed to have long white hair and straggly beards, to be tall and thin, and to wear pointed hats with stars on them. When she finally met Zenith, the WishMaster, she had a shock, because he was like none of these.

For a start he was huge, not fat exactly, just very, very big, and he was completely bald. He wore long, flowing robes, a black cloak like Sebastian's, and in one ear a large gold earring. He stood in front of Maddie with his arms folded and stared down at her from beneath thick, black eyebrows.

Maddie stared back, looking him straight in the eye. The last thing she wanted was for him to think she was afraid of him, even if under her checked shirt her heart was pounding, and inside her jeans her knees were knocking.

"So." His voice really did boom. "You are Madeleine."

Maddie swallowed. "Yes," she said. "But I like to be called Maddie." Might as well get that straight from the very start, she thought.

"Oh, you do, do you!" He seemed surprised, as if he wasn't used to anyone correcting him. "Well, Maddie," he went on and for one moment, although she couldn't be entirely certain because it was gone so quickly, Maddie thought she saw the ghost of a smile on the stern face of the WishMaster. "Sebastian tells me he wants you to go with him on his next Wish assignment. How do you feel about that? Eh?"

"Oh, I would like to go," she replied quickly. "Very much, please."

"Hmm. So what do you think you would be able to do to help? Can't have you hindering the operation, you know. What are you good at? Eh?"

"Well, I don't know really." Maddie began to feel a bit worried, knowing that it was this man who had the power to say whether or not she could go with Sebastian.

It was Zak who intervened. Zak, who had followed Maddie upstairs to Zenith's turret room with its shelves and benches packed with hundreds of dusty books, strange-looking instruments and various pills and sickly-coloured potions. "She might be able to help Sebastian to remember his spells," he said slyly. "You know how hopeless he is at that."

"Hmm, that's a point," said Zenith, stroking his chin. "So are you good at remembering things?"

"Oh yes," Maddie replied eagerly. "I have a very good memory and I learn things very quickly."

"Told you," croaked Zak, flapping his wings excitedly.

Zenith glowered down at Maddie again,

then said, "You'd better stay for the briefing." With that he strode away to the far end of the room beckoning to Sebastian to join him, leaving Maddie with Zak.

"What's a briefing?" whispered Maddie.

"Instructions," the raven muttered back out of the side of his beak. "All the low-down on the unicorn case."

"Oh," said Maddie. "I see." She wasn't sure that she did see, but she hoped things would become clearer.

On the far side of the very large turret room Sebastian seemed to be in deep conversation with the WishMaster. Maddie couldn't hear what they were saying but from Sebastian's actions it was almost as if he was pleading with him.

Maddie turned to Zak again. "Why did Thirza think I would cause trouble with the princess?" she asked curiously.

Zak gave his cackle of a laugh again, but quietly this time so that Zenith wouldn't hear. "The princess is a little madam," he said. "You saw how she considered the little unicorn to be her personal property, well she tends to think of Sebastian in that way as well."

"But that's awful," said Maddie. "No one should own anyone else."

"You try telling the princess that," replied Zak darkly. "She'll be jealous of you, there's no doubt about that, and that's what Thirza meant."

"I can't see why," said Maddie gloomily. "If I looked like she does, I wouldn't be jealous of anyone."

"That's as maybe," said Zak. "But it's you who Sebastian wants to go with him, isn't it? Not Princess Lyra."

Maddie had no time to even consider

this interesting idea, for at that moment, Sebastian and Zenith returned, sweeping across the turret room in a swirl of cloaks.

"I have decided," said Zenith, and Maddie's heart skipped a beat, "that you can accompany Sebastian on this particular assignment. It is very unusual, to say the least, but he is quite insistent that he wants to take you along."

"Oh, thank you," said Maddie. "Thank you very much. I promise I won't be a nuisance."

"Yes, yes, all right." The WishMaster sounded impatient now. "Right," he went on, "sit down the pair of you and listen carefully."

Obediently Maddie and Sebastian sat on a long, low bench facing Zenith while Zak flew across the room and perched on a high wooden rail which looked as if it might have been made especially for him.

"The wish," Zenith began, "has been made by a young unicorn." Sebastian gave Maddie a slight nudge as if warning her not to let on how much they already knew. "Somehow this unicorn must have become separated from his mother and the rest of his herd," Zenith went on. "He was found wandering on the edge of the forest by the Princess Lyra. She brought him back here to the castle but decided not to tell anyone. It was Zak who discovered him one day when he was flying over the royal mews."

"Does the princess look after the little unicorn herself?" asked Sebastian.

"Of course not." It was Zak who replied, after a quick glance to Zenith for approval. "Can you see her mucking out stables?"

"Well, no, not really," Sebastian admitted.

"Exactly," said Zak. "She threatened one of the young grooms with the loss of his job if he refused to look after the little unicorn. I thought this was a dreadful state of affairs," he went on, "what with it being against the law in the first place to keep a unicorn in captivity – so I had a word with the little chap one afternoon when he was on his own."

"What did you say?" breathed Maddie.

"I asked him if he was happy," said Zak with a shrug.

"And was he?" asked Sebastian.

"Nope," said Zak. "Not really. So I put it to him, if he could have one wish, what that wish would be."

"So what did he say?" whispered Maddie.

"He said he wanted to go home to his mother," the raven replied.

There was a long silence in the turret room then Zenith spoke again. "I have decided," he said, "that this is to be an Official Wish, that the young unicorn should be returned to his mother and to the rest of his herd."

"Do we know where the herd are?" asked Sebastian.

"We know they've moved on to new pastures," said Zenith. "It will be your task to find them. I suggest you start off from the point where the unicorn was found."

"But that was on the edge of the Enchanted Forest," said Sebastian.

Zak gave a single squawk and hid his head beneath his wing. Something in Sebastian's voice made Maddie throw him a sidelong glance. To her surprise she saw that his eyes were dark pools of fear.

The WishMaster nodded. "That is correct," he said. "It is also a known fact that the unicorn herd travels through the Enchanted Forest at about the same time each year. The trouble is, and this could be the difficult bit as far as you are concerned, the little unicorn can't remember what happened before he was found – he appears to have lost his memory completely."

Sebastian threw Zak a startled look.

The raven nodded. "That's right," he said. "He can't even remember his own name, let alone what happened to him. The only thing he seems to know is that he wants his mother."

"Could he have been abandoned?" asked Maddie.

"That's a possibility," said the Wish-

Master. "But it seems unlikely. It is very rare for unicorns to abandon their young." He paused, stroking his chin thoughtfully. "What seems more likely," he continued after a moment, "is that something happened on the unicorns' journey through the Enchanted Forest and the little one somehow got separated from them. I think you need to find out what that something was."

No one answered and Maddie thought that Sebastian looked quite pale in spite of the golden brown of his skin.

"Now why are you all looking so glum?" said Zenith. He still sounded impatient.

"There are terrible stories about the Enchanted Forest," said Sebastian. His voice was low and a bit shaky, not like Sebastian's voice at all. "People have disappeared in there, never to be seen again. There are thieves and vagabonds, and the Ice Queen's palace is in the Land of Frost which is not far from the forest." He paused, then for Maddie's benefit he explained, "The Ice Queen is very wicked, and it's said soldiers from her Ice Army patrol the forest at night. . ."

"Aren't you forgetting something!" demanded Zenith, interrupting and drawing himself up to his full height before gazing down at them.

"What's that, Sir?" Sebastian looked up sharply.

"My magic is far superior to anything in the Enchanted Forest and my powers are greater than anything the Ice Queen can produce. . ."

"But you won't be coming with us, will you?" whispered Maddie, her eyes like saucers at all this talk of a wicked Ice

Queen and folk disappearing, never to be seen again.

"Of course I won't be coming with you," boomed Zenith. "The whole point of this exercise is for Sebastian to get more experience, to perform magic and to gain another wish towards winning his Golden Spurs."

The WishMaster drew his robes around him and as they all watched, he turned and unlocked a cabinet on the wall behind him.

"That's where the magic is kept," whispered Sebastian to Maddie. "For one moment there I thought he was going to say we had to try and do this without any magic." When Zenith turned again and walked back to them he was carrying a black casket and two scrolls of parchment bound with red ribbon.

Solemnly he slipped the ribbon from one of the scrolls and with a flourish unrolled it. "You will have two spells to help you with your quest. This," he said, "is the first of the spells. It cannot be allowed to leave this room, so you have to memorize it. When it is used, it has to be word-perfect, otherwise the magic will not work. Is that clear?"

They all nodded but Maddie noticed that Sebastian still looked rather worried.

Zenith cleared his throat, but before he could begin to speak, Maddie took a deep breath and said, "Excuse me. . . ."

Sebastian drew his breath in sharply and The WishMaster stopped and glared at her. "Yes?" he demanded. "What is it now?"

"Please . . . Sebastian did tell me, but I

still don't quite understand" said Maddie in a small voice, "What exactly can the spells do?"

"They can do anything," boomed Zenith. "Anything at all – but it is for Sebastian to use his judgement and decide when they should be used and for what purpose."

"Oh," said Maddie in awe. "Oh, I see." The thought of spells that could do absolutely anything was still really quite amazing.

The WishMaster cleared his throat once again and this time in a grand voice that echoed around the turret room he began reading the words of the spell from the scroll:

"Zamperine from Zedbah,
Zoolery of Zire.

Zad over Zoozecam
Send the Emerald Fire!"

"Oh dear," muttered Sebastian.

"That's all right," said Maddie in relief. "It's quite easy."

"Do you really think so?" Sebastian looked at her in amazement.

"Oh yes," said Maddie. She had been afraid that the spell would be very complicated, but the verse was no more difficult than the poems she learnt at school.

"When you have quite finished talking amongst yourselves," said Zenith sternly, while Zak sniggered from his perch, "I'll give you the second spell."

"But I haven't learnt the first one yet," muttered Sebastian in desperation.

"We'll go over them again." Zenith was

beginning to sound impatient again. He unrolled the second scroll and began to read:

"Zilleriah over Ziskin.
Zanda. Zoska. Zeen.
Zariander of Zillaban
Appear in a Flame of Green!"

"I'll never remember all that," whispered Sebastian, hanging his head in despair.

"It's all right," hissed Maddie reassuringly. "It won't take me long to learn – I promise."

"Now," said Zenith loftily, "all the spells in the world are useless without a conductor of magic." He looked at Maddie. "When Sebastian has won his Golden Spurs he will be presented with his own magic wand," he said, "But he has a long way to go before that. At the moment he is still an apprentice." As he spoke he opened the black casket.

Maddie leaned forward for a better look. Nestling inside the box, on a pad of black velvet, was a ring with a single green stone, a large emerald.

Zenith took the ring from the box, and indicated for Sebastian to stand up. Sebastian moved forward, as he did so slipping the diamond ring he wore from his finger and handing it to the WishMaster. Zenith returned it to the casket before placing the emerald ring on to Sebastian's finger.

Watching, Maddie suddenly felt so proud of Sebastian that she thought she might burst.

Sebastian lifted his hand and, caught

in a shaft of sunlight which streamed
through one of the tiny panes of glass, the
stone seemed to flash green fire.

"It's beautiful," breathed Maddie in awe.

"This time you carry the power of the emerald with you. You must not get carried away by this power," said Zenith in his solemn, booming voice. "You must have respect for the emerald and for the spells, you must not use either lightly, and you must always remember that for each of the wishes you grant, you have only two spells to help you."

He paused. "Use the spells wisely," he commanded. "You will be answerable to me, Sebastian, and you will be judged on how you choose to use the powers you have been given. But remember," he paused, "after you have used both spells, you are on your own."

There was silence in the turret room following the WishMaster's words. It was broken only when Zenith himself spoke again, but this time his tone was less solemn, softer, almost kindly.

"Let's go through the spells again," he said. "Afterwards, you will eat the meal Thirza has prepared, and then, you must be on your way."

Chapter Six

The Enchanted Forest

"It isn't really dreadful in the Enchanted Forest, is it Zak?" asked Maddie fearfully. It was a little later and she and the raven were waiting for Sebastian, who had gone into the royal mews to fetch the baby unicorn.

"Are you kidding?" Zak flapped his wings. "Last time I went in there I came out with all my feathers on end. It's dead creepy."

"Oh dear," said Maddie anxiously. She was quite brave really when it came to some things but she wasn't too sure about creepy. At that moment their attention was taken by Sebastian, who came out of the stable leading the little unicorn by a red, plaited cord that he had tied around its neck.

"We need to go straight away," he said. "Apparently the Princess Lyra is making a terrible fuss. I think we should go before she gets back. I don't want another scene."

"I bet you don't," cackled Zak. "And boy, will she make a scene when she knows Zenith has said Maddie can come with us."

"And you can be quiet," said Sebastian, "otherwise we'll leave you behind."

They were all silent after that as together they left the royal mews and hurried through the royal gardens. With the little unicorn trotting beside them they crossed the drawbridge, with Zak muttering at the guards, and took a narrow pathway through the cornfields.

There was no sign of the Princess Lyra but just to be on the safe side they didn't stop until they were well clear of the castle. Then in the shelter of a clump of tall trees with silvery leaves they paused, so that Sebastian could question the little unicorn.

"Can you remember anything at all?" he asked gently.

"Not really," the little unicorn replied. "I can remember wandering around on the edge of the forest. I only know I was looking for my mother and I couldn't find her anywhere. Then I saw two children playing."

"Was one of them the Princess Lyra?" asked Maddie.

The little unicorn nodded. "I didn't know that at the time, of course, neither did I know that the boy with her was her brother."

"The Crown Prince Frederic," explained Sebastian.

"A silly fat boy who does nothing but stuff himself with sweets," sniffed Zak. "I reckon he—"

"Zak. . ." said Sebastian warningly.

"OK!" Zak lapsed into silence.

"So what happened next?" Sebastian turned his attention to the little unicorn again.

"The princess said she wanted to keep me," he replied. "Her brother told her it was against the law but she said she didn't care. They took me back to the castle and the princess put me in her play house behind the royal mews. She ordered one of the grooms to look after me. He seemed too frightened of her to refuse."

"Why did she want you if she didn't even want to look after you?" asked Maddie, thinking of her own pet, Whisker, and of how she loved to feed the cat and play with her.

"She said she would keep me until I'd grown up," the little unicorn replied. "Then she said she would ride on my back and show off to her friends who only had ordinary ponies."

"That sounds like the princess," squawked Zak from a perch amongst the silvery leaves.

"Was she kind to you?" asked Maddie anxiously.

"Sort of," said the little unicorn. "But she doesn't really know anything about unicorns and I was unhappy because I only wanted to be with my mother. Then one day Zak came to see me." He glanced up at the raven who nodded down at him. "He asked me what I would wish for if I had only one wish in the world."

"And you said to be with your mother again," breathed Maddie, as the tears filled her eyes.

"But how can I?" said the little unicorn sadly, "When I can't remember what happened?"

"Maybe you need to go back to the forest," said Sebastian. "Perhaps you will remember then."

"Maybe." The little unicorn nodded,

but Maddie didn't think he sounded too sure and she noticed little drops of moisture had formed on his brow and were beginning to trickle down his face.

Sebastian stood up and looked around as if he was trying to get his bearings. Then at last, he pointed into the distance. "That's the forest," he said, "over there to the north."

Maddie looked in the direction in which he was pointing and saw, beyond the bright yellow of the cornfields, a mass of trees so dense that from this distance they looked almost black. In spite of the warmth from the sun she felt herself shiver.

They began to walk again, trudging through the fields in single file towards the forest, Sebastian leading the way,

Maddie in the centre, then the little unicorn, and Zak flying in the rear.

At last they reached the fringes of the forest. "Keep together," called Sebastian warily. His voice sounded almost harsh in the stillness. The trees were quite sparse to start with and sunlight filtered through the branches, but the further they went the closer the trees grew together and the darker it became, until at last the sunlight couldn't penetrate at all.

The little unicorn was very quiet, then suddenly he stopped and began pawing the soft ground as if he were getting agitated.

"What is it?" asked Sebastian in a low voice. "Do you remember anything?"

"I don't know . . . I'm not sure." The little unicorn looked around, his eyes rolling. "I think something terrible happened here, but I don't remember what it was."

"I think we should go on a bit further," said Sebastian.

Zak, who had also been remarkably quiet, gave a muted little squawk then began twittering nervously as they all moved forward down a pathway, where the branches of the trees met overhead forming a cool, green tunnel.

"Shut up, Zak," said Sebastian, but even he sounded nervous now. Zak fell silent and the only sound to be heard was the soft thud of the little unicorn's hooves.

They walked on for what seemed like miles, peering from left to right as they went, but all they could see was the dense darkness of the trees.

It grew colder and suddenly Maddie stopped. It was so sudden that the little unicorn almost crashed into her. Zak began squawking and flapping and Sebastian stopped and looked back to see what the commotion was about.

"What is it?" he said. "What's wrong?"

"It's the trees," said Maddie.

"What's wrong with 'em?" muttered Zak nervously.

"They . . . they keep moving or something . . . they shouldn't because there isn't any wind."

"What do you mean, *moving?*" Sebastian stared round uneasily at the trees which were so still they appeared motionless.

"I don't know," said Maddie. "It's when we're walking. It's almost as if they were creeping nearer. I'm sure the pathway is getting narrower."

"It's your imagination," said Zak, but even he didn't sound his usual cocksure self.

They carried on but they'd only gone a few more yards when Maddie gave a sudden shriek.

"Oh, for goodness sake, what is it now?" squawked Zak, leaping into the air then hovering overhead.

"The branches," cried Maddie. "Look, they're like tentacles – I'm sure that one tried to grab hold of me." She pointed to a long, snake-like branch that trailed across the path.

"I think we are all getting tired," said Sebastian, "and when you are tired your mind can play funny tricks. I know you need to rest, but I think we'd better press on a bit further."

The friends gritted their teeth and,

trying hard to ignore any terrors that might be lurking amongst the trees, they carried on.

"We know the herd came through the forest," said Sebastian a little later, "so maybe we'll find some clues to where they are now."

But it only grew colder and darker the deeper they went into the forest. Time and again Maddie thought she sensed movements amongst the trees, until at last there came a point when she could bear it no longer. "How much further do we have to go?" she wailed.

"I'm not sure," Sebastian admitted. "We certainly haven't seen anything yet to suggest that the herd even came this way."

"Can't you use a spell or something to get us out?" Maddie was close to tears. "I

think we're going round in circles. That tree we saw just now, I'm sure we passed it before. It was grinning at us."

"Don't be silly," said Zak. "Trees don't grin."

"This one did," choked Maddie. "It had a face, a horrible face, and it grinned at me, I tell you. I'm cold, Sebastian, I don't like it, I want to go home."

"I don't really want to use a spell, not yet." Sebastian sounded worried and even he looked scared now. "It's far too soon," he went on, "and if we did it would only leave us with one. We could have a long way to go yet."

"You've forgotten it, haven't you?" Maddie gave a loud hiccup. "Well, I haven't, I can remember it." And she began chanting:

"Zamperine from Zedbah,
Zoolery of—"

But Sebastian wasn't listening to her, instead he had lifted his head and appeared to be straining his ears, listening to something else.

"Be quiet, Maddie," he said sharply. "Listen, can you hear that noise?"

"What noise?" Maddie gulped, and they all froze in the darkness.

"That noise," said Sebastian.

They all heard it then, a steady thudding noise.

"What do you think it is?" said Zak uncertainly, while the little unicorn gave a whimper.

"I don't know," muttered Sebastian.

"Danger!" the little unicorn snorted, his nostrils flaring with fear.

113

"Well, I don't know about you guys."
Zak flapped his wings. "But I'm out of
here!"

Chapter Seven

The Woodcutter's Wife

"So am I," gasped Maddie.

"And me," squealed the little unicorn.

With Zak flying alongside they turned and fled back down the path.

A sudden stern shout from Sebastian brought them crashing to a halt. "Where do you think you're going?" he demanded.

Sheepishly they looked round.

"It's no earthly good you lot disappearing at the first sign of trouble," he said coldly. "On the other hand, if you can't cope, then maybe it would be best if you went back now. I'll carry on alone with the little unicorn."

"No, Sebastian," said Maddie shamefaced. "I'm sorry. I'll come with you."

"Yeah, all right," said Zak, "I guess that means me and all."

"In that case," Sebastian's voice still sounded cold, "instead of running away like a bunch of cowards, we first need to establish exactly what that noise is."

They crept forward, deeper into the forest, and all the while the thudding grew louder, and closer.

"Maddie," the little unicorn nudged her shoulder, "I don't like it. What do you think it is?"

"I don't know," Maddie gulped. "I just wish Sebastian would use a spell."

"Perhaps you should make that an Official Wish," croaked Zak over her other shoulder.

"Oh," whispered Maddie. "Do you think I could?"

"Trouble with that is you'd have to go all the way back and clear it with Zenith first," Zak replied.

"Will you lot please be quiet!" snapped Sebastian suddenly.

"Sorry," said Maddie, then quite by chance, she glanced to her left through the trees. She stopped and stared. "Oh, I say," she whispered. "Look down there."

They all stopped then and looked to where the land dipped away to form a hollow like a large basin. At the bottom of the hollow was a cottage, a funny, twisty

little cottage with ivy-covered walls and a red tiled roof. Smoke was rising from the one chimney in a long, thin column, and in front of the cottage a man was chopping logs and stacking them into a huge pile. Every time the axe hit the wood the thud echoed around the hollow.

"That's it," said Sebastian, and there was a definite note of relief in his voice. "That's the noise we could hear."

"A woodcutter," said Zak. With that he spread his wings, flapped a few times, then glided down into the hollow and perched on the pile of logs.

The man stopped what he was doing and said something to Zak. The raven must have told him that the others were watching because the man turned then and looked up into the forest.

"Come on," said Sebastian. "We'd better

go down. Maybe he'll be able to tell us something."

They tumbled helter-skelter down the steep bank into the hollow, slipping and sliding as they went, until they landed almost in a heap before the man.

"These are my friends," said Zak. "Sebastian, Maddie who is from the Other Place, and the little unicorn."

The man laid down his axe and eyed them up and down. His hair was as white as snow, his face lined and weather-beaten, but his eyes were kind and they twinkled beneath bushy white eyebrows. "What brings you into the forest?" he asked, looking from one to the other of them.

"We're looking for the unicorn herd." It was Sebastian who answered.

"Unicorn herd, you say?" The wood-cutter frowned.

"Have you seen them?" Maddie's red curls bobbed furiously as she leaned forward and gazed up into his face.

He shook his head. "Not recently," he said. "But I know they travel through the forest." He looked curiously at the little unicorn. "So what's your name?" he asked.

"We don't know," Sebastian explained. "You see, we think he was with the herd when something happened right here in the forest. The problem is he's lost his memory so he can't remember what happened."

"Lost his memory you say?" The woodcutter looked startled. "That's strange," he said slowly. "My wife has also lost her memory."

"Your wife?" Sebastian looked past the man and through the open door of the cottage.

"Yes," said the man. "It happened one night when she went out into the forest to collect herbs – they have to be collected when the moon is rising, you see."

"So what happened?" said Sebastian urgently, while Zak flapped his wings in excitement.

"I don't know." The woodcutter shook his head. "She didn't come home. I got worried and went to look for her. "

"Did you find her?" asked Maddie anxiously.

"Oh yes, I found her eventually," he replied grimly. "She was right in the heart of the forest lying in some undergrowth. The trees and bushes all around her had been bent and trampled on."

"So what had happened to her?" squawked Zak.

"Goodness knows," said the woodcutter.

"She was in a bad way, I can tell you. She was stone cold, and not only did she not know who I was, she didn't even know her own name. I carried her home and put her to bed, where she has been ever since. She is very weak and I fear she grows weaker every day. She's never regained her memory and she is still cold. So cold you would hardly believe it," he added sadly.

"Can we see her?" asked Maddie gently.

"Well," said the woodcutter, "I suppose it'll be all right, but she really is very poorly."

While Zak and the little unicorn waited outside, Sebastian and Maddie followed the woodcutter into the cottage.

The man's wife was lying on a narrow bed under the window. Her face was very pale, her grey hair untidy and straggly. The man knelt by her side and took her hand.

"These people are looking for the unicorn herd," he said. "They have a little unicorn with them who has lost his memory, just like you."

The woman opened her eyes and gazed

dully at Maddie and Sebastian.

"Can you remember anything at all about that night in the forest?" asked Maddie, sinking to her knees beside the bed.

The woman's eyes darkened and drops of sweat broke out on her forehead. "I'm not sure I should even try to think about it," she said. "My husband has told me that all my troubles began that night – this weakness in my legs, so bad now that I can scarcely move . . . and the cold, cold like I've never known. I'm sorry, I can't help you."

"We'd best go, Maddie," murmured Sebastian in her ear. "We mustn't trouble this poor lady any further." Putting one hand under Maddie's elbow he helped her to her feet.

They had almost reached the door when the woman suddenly called out to them. "Did you say you have a unicorn with you who has also lost his memory?"

"Yes." Maddie turned eagerly.

"Let me see him," said the woman weakly.

Sebastian hurried outside, returning a moment later leading the little unicorn by the red plaited cord.

The woodcutter's wife moved her head to look at him, then the next moment her eyes had widened and she was struggling to raise herself up.

"You were there that night," she gasped as she gazed at the little unicorn. "I saw you, you were with your mother and the rest of your herd. . ."

"She's remembering!" whispered the woodcutter as at that moment Zak hopped into the room and perched on the brass rail at the foot of the bed.

"You unicorns were moving so gracefully through the forest in the moonlight, so proud and dignified," the woodcutter's wife went on slowly.

"So what happened?" urged Sebastian. "Can you remember?"

"She came," muttered the woman, her eyes darkening with fear. "She came with her soldiers. . ."

"Who?" breathed Maddie, clasping her hands together in fright.

"Yes, who?" said Sebastian kneeling beside the bed and taking one of the woman's hands in his.

"Her," whispered the woodcutter's wife. "The Ice Queen!"

A shudder, like a chill wind, seemed to ripple through the room.

"The soldiers descended on the forest like a plague of locusts," she continued after a moment, "and the poor unicorns scattered. The crashing and stamping and squealing was terrible. I've never heard such sounds and I hope I never do again. Your mother told you to run," she said, looking at the little unicorn. "She said, 'Run, Peregrine, run!'"

"Oh," exclaimed Maddie, turning to the little unicorn, sinking to her knees and slipping her arms around his neck. "Is that your name – Peregrine?"

"Yes," he replied as she kissed the tip of his nose. "It is, and I did run. I remember now. Oh, I remember! I ran and ran until I couldn't run any more . . . but. . . Oh," he looked over Maddie's shoulder to the woodcutter's wife again, "do you know what happened after I'd gone?"

"She was shrieking at her soldiers," said the woman, "ordering them to capture a unicorn to draw her chariot."

Zak gave a tiny squawk and hid his head under one wing, and the little unicorn whimpered in fear.

Only Maddie was bewildered. "Who is this Ice Queen?" she demanded, sitting back on her heels. "Why is everyone so afraid of her, for goodness' sake?"

"She's wicked," said the woodcutter simply. "An evil, wicked woman."

"Tell us, please, what happened next," Sebastian said gently to the woman on the bed.

The woman closed her eyes for a moment, then took a deep breath, as if summoning the last of her strength.

Maddie felt Peregrine nuzzle his face into her back, as if by doing so he could shut out the terrible images of that night that the return of his memory had restored to him.

There was silence in the room, a tense silence as everyone waited for the woman to continue her story.

"I saw her quite clearly," she continued at last. "She was mounted on her white stallion. The unicorns were terrified and there was a lot more squealing and crashing about as the soldiers chased them and they scattered. After I heard the mother tell the little one to run, she turned to face the Ice Soldiers. I think she thought that if she could delay them in some way, he would have a better chance to escape. But in doing that she sealed her own fate. You see, the others got away, but she was the one they took."

Exhausted from the effort of telling her story, she lay back against her pillows and closed her eyes.

"But where is she now?" cried Peregrine.

"Where did they take my mother?"

"To the Ice Palace," said the woman. "After the soldiers had captured her, the Ice Queen rode up and said that she was the one, that she would be perfect for what she wanted."

"Did the Ice Queen see you watching?" asked Zak suddenly.

"Yes." The woman gave a deep sigh. "She stared straight at me. I think she may have put a curse on me. She froze my memory and my legs. And I think little Peregrine might have caught the tail end of that curse." With a sigh she turned to her husband who took her hand.

"Anna, my dearest," he said.

"That's terrible," said Maddie, shocked by what she had just heard.

"So Peregrine's mother has been kidnapped," said Zak thoughtfully. "And even now she is a prisoner of the Ice Queen."

"Where does the Ice Queen live?" asked Maddie.

"At the Ice Palace," replied the woodcutter. "It's to the north, on the far side of the Enchanted Forest in the Land of Frost."

"It makes me feel cold just to think of it," said Maddie with a shiver, then looking at Sebastian, she said, "What are we going to do?"

"Our mission was to grant Peregrine's wish," said Sebastian slowly. "His wish was to be returned to his mother. He wouldn't want to be a prisoner of the Ice Queen, would you, Peregrine?" He glanced down at the little unicorn.

"Oh, no," said Peregrine. "But I do want to be with my mother Phoebe again . . .

and Cornelius my father, and the rest of my herd."

"So there's only one thing to be done," said Sebastian firmly. "We have to rescue Peregrine's mother from the Ice Palace and then return both of them to the herd."

"Oh boy!" said Zak.

The woodcutter shook his head sadly as if he considered this to be an impossible mission.

His wife opened her eyes. "How can you hope to overcome the evil of the Ice Queen?" she said.

Swirling his cloak around him Sebastian drew himself up to his full height. "The Ice Queen may have powers of her own," he said haughtily, "but I also have magic power, and I believe my magic to be greater than hers."

"Wicked!" squawked Zak. "That's right, my son, you tell 'em!"

After resting for most of the night and sharing a simple meal with the woodcutter and his wife, the friends were on their way before first light, heading north through the forest to the Land of Frost and the Ice Palace. They travelled mostly without talking, and in the end it was Maddie who broke the silence.

"Sebastian," she said, "I'm worried about Peregrine's mother, but I can't stop thinking about that poor woman."

He stopped. "The woodcutter's wife?" he said. "I know, neither can I."

"What do you think will become of her?" said Maddie fearfully.

"With the curse of the Ice Queen upon her – she will surely grow colder and slowly freeze to death."

"Oh dear," said Maddie. She was silent again, then after a while she said, "Didn't you say you believed your magic to be stronger than that of the Ice Queen?"

"Yes." Sebastian nodded.

"So isn't there anything you could do?"

"I've already thought of that," said Sebastian. "And yes, I could do something. But it would mean using one of our spells."

"Well then. . ." said Maddie.

"If I was alone, I wouldn't hesitate," Sebastian replied. "But there are four of us to think of here, and we may be facing many more dangers yet. . ."

"I still think we should do something to help her," said Maddie. "After all, she's helped us. If it wasn't for her we wouldn't know what had happened, would we?"

"I think we should help her too," said Peregrine suddenly. "It's thanks to her I've got my memory back."

"You can count me in on that," said Zak.

Sebastian turned away from them and stood a little apart. He looked so alone that Maddie felt sorry for him. She wanted to go to him, to help him in some way, but before she could move he turned back to them again.

"You are all agreed?" he said and they nodded vigorously.

"In that case. . ." He took a deep breath and looked up. The moon was still up and Sebastian lifted his hand so that the emerald ring shone in the silvery light. Watched by the others, slowly, carefully, he began to chant the spell:

"Zamperine from Zedbah,
Zoolery of Zire.
Zad over Zoolecam
Send—"

"Zecam," interrupted Maddie.

"What?" said Sebastian.

"It's zecam," she said. "Zad over Zoozecam."

"That's what I said," retorted Sebastian.

"No," said Maddie. "You didn't. You said Zad over Zoolecam. It has to be right, Sebastian. You know what Zenith said. If it isn't word perfect the spell won't work."

"She's right," said Zak.

"Oh, very well," said Sebastian. "Zad over Zoozecam, then.

"Send—"

"I think you should say the whole thing again," said Maddie in a small voice.

Sebastian looked annoyed and for one moment Maddie thought he was going to refuse.

"Shall I say it with you?" she asked in the same small voice.

Sebastian hesitated.

"It's got to be right, old son," said Zak. "I'd let her if I were you."

"All right," Sebastian said at last with a little shrug. Then together, he and Maddie repeated the whole spell over again.

"*Zamperine from Zedbah,*
Zoolery of Zire.
Zad over Zoozecam
Send the Emerald Fire!"

Then as the emerald ring shone in the moonlight, he said, "May the curse of the

Ice Queen be lifted from the wood-cutter's wife."

There was a sudden blinding flash of green fire before the moon disappeared behind a cloud, and they were plunged into darkness.

"How do you know whether or not it has worked?" whispered Peregrine.

"It will have worked," said Sebastian calmly. "No doubt about that."

"Oh Sebastian," said Maddie, admiringly.

"And now," he said, "we must travel onwards to the Palace of the Ice Queen to fulfil our mission."

Chapter Eight

The Land of Frost

It grew steadily colder through the remainder of the night as they travelled further north, and in time Maddie was shivering and her teeth were chattering.

"You're cold," said Sebastian and taking off his long black cloak, he put it round her shoulders. It was too long because Sebastian was much taller than her, but it was blissfully warm. "Is that better?" he asked.

"Oh yes," sighed Maddie. "But what about you? You'll be cold now."

"I don't feel the cold," said Sebastian.

Maddie suspected he was only saying that to make her feel better. "What about the others?" she said, glancing back.

"They're all right," said Sebastian. "Zak has his feathers to keep him warm and Peregrine has a thick coat."

Much later, as the sky began to lighten with the dawn, Maddie said, "Do you think it's much further to the Ice Palace?"

"I don't know." Sebastian looked round. "But I think we must be getting close. It's much colder, and look at those trees – their twigs are icicles and the leaves aren't leaves at all, they are snowflakes."

"They are very beautiful," said Maddie,

reaching out and touching one of the icicles with her finger only to draw back sharply. "It's so cold," she gasped, "it almost burns."

"A bit like the Ice Queen herself," said Sebastian grimly. "Beautiful, but deadly."

"How about I fly on and see how much further we have to go?" asked Zak suddenly.

"Good idea," said Sebastian. "But don't let anyone see you. A black raven stands out in this white landscape."

"OK," said Zak and spreading his wings he took off gliding away through the icy trees.

They walked on following the same path, the only sounds an occasional cracking from Peregrine's hooves when he trod on a frozen puddle and the lonely, desolate whistle of the wind in the trees.

Zak didn't return and when Maddie voiced fears about his safety, Sebastian simply shrugged. "If anyone can take care of himself, it's Zak," he said. But Maddie still worried and longed to see the familiar shape of the raven swoop down out of the sky and join them again.

After a time the trees began to thin out on one side of the path and they could see a huge lake which appeared to be covered entirely with ice.

And then quite suddenly, at the far end of the lake, glittering in the pale dawn light, a palace seemed to rise up out of the early morning mist. Its walls and battlements looked as if they were made entirely from glass, while hundreds of turrets and pinnacles soared upwards and seemed to pierce the very sky.

"The Ice Palace!" Sebastian's breath

hung in the cold air and for a long moment they stood and stared.

It reminded Maddie of a picture she had once seen in a book, of a palace in a fairytale, but before she had the chance to say as much, a loud whirring sound filled the air followed by a flapping of wings. Zak had returned.

"You need to hide," he rasped. "Ice Soldiers – coming this way!"

"Quick," said Sebastian. "Behind the bushes."

They dived off the pathway and crouched down in the long frosty grass behind a great mass of silver and white bushes. They were only just in time, for almost immediately they heard the steady tramp-tramping sound of boots marching on the frozen pathway.

Holding their breath and hardly daring

to move, the friends watched as soldiers from the Ice Army passed by right in front of their noses.

The soldiers were tall and wore tunics of pale ice-blue, they carried round silver shields but everything else about them seemed pointed: pointed helmets and spears, pointed toes to their boots, and gauntlets with pointed fingers. Even their ears and noses looked long and pointed.

"They look really weird," Maddie whispered to Sebastian as the last of the battalion disappeared from view on its way to the Ice Palace.

"You realize they're made entirely of ice, don't you?" Sebastian whispered back.

"Made of ice?" squeaked Maddie.

"Shush!" said Zak. "That was the night patrol. Heaven help anyone they find in the forest."

"What would happen to them?" said Peregrine in a very small voice.

"They'd take 'em back to the palace and they'd never be seen again, that's what!"

"Like my mother?" said Peregrine fearfully.

"Quite," said Zak. Then hastily, as the little unicorn's eyes filled with tears, he added, "'Cept that you will be seeing your mum again, 'cos we're going to get her out."

"What happens in the summer?" asked Maddie curiously.

"What do you mean 'in the summer'?" said Sebastian with a frown.

"To the soldiers. You said they were made of ice, so what happens to them in the summer when the sun shines? Do they melt?"

"The sun never shines in the Land of Frost," said Sebastian. "It's always winter."

Maddie was shocked at such an idea. The thought of no sunshine, no summer, no flowers and no trips to the seaside was too awful even to imagine.

"All this nattering is all very well," said Zak suddenly, sternly. "But has anyone given any thought as to how we are actually going to get inside this place?"

"The second spell?" Peregrine suggested hopefully.

"I'd rather save it," said Sebastian. "We may well need it to get out."

"So what then?" said Maddie.

"It's a fortress of a place," said Zak. "It's built entirely of ice – the walls are several feet thick."

"Is there a moat?" asked Maddie, remembering the moat around the royal castle.

"No." Zak shook his head. "Wouldn't

be a lot of good if there was. Moats are meant to keep people out, but if there was one here it would be frozen solid so anyone could simply skate over it."

"Right," said Sebastian, "so if there's no moat, what have they got to keep folk out?"

"Just the soldiers," said Zak. "But there are hundreds of 'em. They guard the entrances and patrol the walls all the time."

"So how on earth are we going to get past them?" asked Maddie in dismay.

"Presumably supplies have to go into the Ice Palace?" said Sebastian thoughtfully.

"Yes," said Zak. "I saw a cart full of provisions go in through a small gateway at the side."

"That could be it," said Sebastian. He

spoke slowly but there was no mistaking the excitement in his voice. "That could be our way in. Come on." He turned towards the Ice Palace. "Let's go."

They approached very cautiously, creeping forward, running from bush to bush, from one belt of trees to another. All seemed quiet, but just when they thought it might be safe to make a final dash to the palace, the main gates opened and a group of the Ice Soldiers marched out.

"Wait!" Sebastian held the friends back and they hid behind some bushes, their hearts pounding with fear. The soldiers changed places with those on duty at the gates, who were duly escorted back inside the palace walls.

"Right," said Zak, when the gates closed

once more, "what we need to do now is get round to the side and find that other entrance. The one I saw the supplies go through. Follow me."

With Zak flying very low the friends followed him, skirting the walls of the huge building, and finally making a dash for a huge clump of rocks.

At last, puffing and panting, they flung themselves down behind the snow-covered rocks.

"That's it!" croaked Zak. "There's the gate!" They peered round the rocks and saw the other, smaller entrance.

"There are guards on that gate as well," Peregrine pointed out.

"What happened, Zak, when you saw the supply cart arrive?" asked Sebastian thoughtfully.

"It slowed right down," said Zak. "The

guards spoke to the driver before waving him on through the gates."

"Good," said Sebastian and they all looked at him in surprise. "That is what I hoped. Now listen, this is what we'll do. When the next cart comes along and the guards are talking to the driver, Maddie and myself will sneak out from behind these rocks, make a dash for the back of the cart, climb aboard and hide amongst the supplies."

"What if the soldiers want to see inside the cart?" asked Maddie dubiously.

"Hopefully they won't," said Zak.

"What about me?" asked Peregrine.

"I want you to stay here with Zak," said Sebastian.

Maddie saw Peregrine's face fall. "Oh," he said. "Can't I come with you?"

"No, Peregrine," said Sebastian. "I really

don't think that would be a very good idea. You know how the Ice Queen is about unicorns. It would only need someone to get a glimpse of you and you would be marched off to her stables to join your mother – then we would have two of you to rescue. Besides, we may be glad of having you and Zak outside the walls. We might need help to get out."

They had a long wait amongst the rocks. Nothing seemed to be happening. The gates remained firmly shut, but they could quite clearly see the soldiers who patrolled the ramparts and around the base of the palace walls.

"Maybe they've had all their supplies for today," whispered Maddie. She was feeling very stiff and cramped from sitting in one position for so long and her eyes ached with the glare of the bright light from all the ice and snow. She was beginning to think that maybe waiting for another cart wasn't such a good idea after all.

And then, just when they had almost given up hope, Zak suddenly cocked his head on one side.

"Listen!" he snapped.

Maddie strained her ears and, sure enough, she could hear the steady thud of horses' hooves approaching the Ice Palace.

"Sounds like we're in business," said Sebastian excitedly. "Now, everyone knows what they have to do? Maddie?"

"Oh, yes," she answered.

They waited in an agony of suspense as the sound of the hooves grew closer, and then, racing across the icy wastes, there came into view not the horse and cart of a supply merchant, as they had expected, but a slim, elegant, racing chariot, driven by a tall woman swathed in furs.

"The Ice Queen!" muttered Sebastian with a shudder, as the woman cracked her whip and the poor animal that drew her chariot reared and whinnied in terror.

Even from their hiding place they could see that the beast's eyes were rolling, its nostrils wide with fear, and it was then, as the chariot streaked past them, that Maddie realized this was no ordinary horse. It was a magnificent animal, white as snow and with a flowing mane. Its flanks were flecked with foam but from its forehead there protruded a single, long, twisted horn.

"It's my mother!" cried Peregrine and it was only Sebastian's quick thinking in clapping his hand over the little unicorn's mouth to silence him, and grabbing the

red plaited cord around his neck, that
stopped him from rushing forward out of
their hiding place to join her.

Another crack from the Ice Queen's whip filled the air like a pistol shot and the friends were all forced to help restrain Peregrine and calm him down. Then with his eyes rolling and his neck arched he watched helplessly as the Ice Guards opened the gates, the chariot streaked through, and the gates closed behind it once more.

"We'll get her out, Peregrine, I promise," said Sebastian desperately.

"But how. . .?" Peregrine sounded close to despair now, and even Maddie was beginning to feel that theirs could be a hopeless quest.

There was no time for further talk, however, because almost before the sounds of the chariot had died away they were replaced by the noise of another arrival – yet more hoofbeats, but slower

this time and accompanied by loud rumbling and creaking sounds.

"This could be it!" said Sebastian, and they all held their breath in suspense.

And indeed it was, for even as they watched, a cart drawn by a very elderly horse, and driven by an equally elderly man, trundled into view.

The four friends watched in silence as the cart passed by only a few feet from where they were hiding. Then, as it shuddered to a halt before the gates of the Ice Palace, Sebastian issued his command.

"Right, Maddie?" he said. "Then go, now!"

Leaving Sebastian's cloak behind, afraid it might slow her down, Maddie bent almost double and ran after him towards the cart.

"Come on, quick." He lifted the canvas sheet and helped her scramble aboard.

It was dark inside the cart as Sebastian pulled the cover over them both. There was also a strange smell from the lumpy objects they found themselves lying on.

"So what've you got this time, then?" said a gruff voice from outside.

Maddie and Sebastian stiffened, and listened as one of the guards walked to the back of the cart.

"Only cabbages," muttered the driver. "Nothing to get excited about."

"How do we know that's all you've got?" said the guard in the same harsh voice.

"Oh no!" whispered Maddie as someone began fumbling with the canvas cover.

"Burrow in the cabbages," hissed Sebastian. "As deep as you can."

Just when it seemed certain they would

be discovered, there came a whirring and a flapping sound from outside, followed by a loud squawking, then muffled shouts from the guards.

"Get off! Get that creature off me! Go away! Clear off, you wretched bird!"

"Zak!" breathed Sebastian. He clutched Maddie's hand and in the darkness she could see his eyes gleaming. Then there came a sudden lurch and the cart began to rumble forward.

Moments later the cart stopped but Maddie and Sebastian, almost afraid to breathe, kept very, very still.

At long last Sebastian spoke. "I'm going to have a look," he whispered.

"Please be careful," Maddie whispered back.

He lifted a corner of the canvas and peered out. "Well," he said, "we're certainly inside the palace. I can see the gates and they are shut. I don't know where the driver has gone, but I think we'd better get out before he comes back and starts to unload his goods."

Cautiously they climbed out of the cart, Sebastian helping Maddie as she jumped to the ground. She wasn't sorry to leave the cabbages as their smell really was getting very strong.

They found themselves in a courtyard surrounded by high walls and buildings.

"We need to find the stables," said Sebastian in a low voice. "I guess that's where they would keep Peregrine's mother."

"That looks like stables over there." Maddie pointed to the far side of the courtyard. "Look, you can see horses in there."

"Yes, but there are also soldiers about,"

whispered Sebastian. "I don't think we should go straight across. I suggest we go round the outside."

Together they carefully began to skirt the vast courtyard, keeping well within the shadows of the tall buildings.

They passed one large, lighted room crouching low as they ran for fear of being seen. The sound of voices came from the room, voices and laughter and what sounded like the noise of people eating and drinking from metal plates and tankards.

"I expect someone's giving the driver something to eat," whispered Maddie.

"With a bit of luck no one will notice us," said Sebastian. Then taking Maddie's hand he added, "Come on, one last dash and we can make it to the stables."

With their heads down they ran,

slipping and sliding on the cobbled ground but not stopping until they had reached the long, low building of the stable block and dived inside.

There were horses in most of the stalls, and all were the purest white. One or two of them whickered softly as the friends approached.

Sebastian paused and looked around. The strong smell of horse filled the air together with the sweeter smell of fresh hay and the unmistakable tang of leather. "Where is she?" he murmured. "Where is Phoebe?"

A couple of the horses began to move about, pawing the ground and making anxious little noises.

"Phoebe?" called Sebastian in a loud whisper. Silence followed, then from the far end of the stable block there came the unmistakable sound of a loud whinny.

"I think she's through there," whispered Maddie.

"Come on." Sebastian led the way past dozens of stalls to one that stood on its own, apart from the others, at the very end of the block. There were bars at the top of this stall where all the others were open, but peering through the bars, proud and dignified, her neck arched, her mane flowing, her eyes rolling with excitement, was the beautiful white unicorn.

"Phoebe," cried Sebastian, "we've come to rescue you!" Stretching out his hand he reached through the bars and stroked her face. "I am Sebastian," he went on. "This is my friend Maddie. Zak the raven is outside . . . and Peregrine is with him."

"Peregrine! Peregrine is with you?"
There was no disguising Phoebe's delight
at the mention of her son.

"It was Peregrine who brought about the
rescue," said Sebastian. "He made a wish

to Zenith, the WishMaster, to be returned to you. It was our job to find you. It's now my job to grant the wish."

"Sebastian." He looked down as Maddie urgently tugged his sleeve.

"What is it?" he said and she thought he sounded impatient again.

"There's a padlock on the door."

Together they stared in dismay at the huge padlock that bound the door with thick chains.

"You'll need the key," said Phoebe.

"So where is it?" Sebastian looked round at the halters, saddles and bridles hanging from the walls.

"She has it." Phoebe gave a snort of fear. "The Ice Queen. She wears it on a chain around her waist."

"Then we have to get it," said Sebastian calmly.

"She won't let you have it." Phoebe rolled her eyes. "She won't let anyone have it."

"We'll see about that," said Sebastian. "Now, where do we find the Ice Queen?"

"She'll be in the throne room," said Phoebe. "But Sebastian, you must be careful or she'll take you both captive. She'll make you her servants."

"Huh," Sebastian drew himself up and folded his arms. "I'd like to see her try!"

"Don't!" said Phoebe. "She's a very evil woman. All her servants are young people who have been kidnapped from the villages around the Enchanted Forest. Once in the clutches of the Ice Queen they say there is no chance of escape."

"Well, we'll see about that," said Sebastian again while Maddie stared at him, wide-eyed now with fear at what she had just heard. "So how do we get to this throne room?"

"It is upstairs," said Phoebe, while the other horses began to whicker and paw the ground. "At the very top of the palace. Oh, but please, please take care. Promise me you'll take care."

"Of course we will," said Sebastian airily. "It takes more than the evil of the Ice Queen to scare us, doesn't it, Maddie?"

Maddie gulped, unable to answer him because her teeth had started to chatter. Then with a final, fearful, backward glance to Phoebe, who rolled her eyes once more, she ran after Sebastian as he strode back through the stable block and outside into the courtyard.

Chapter Nine

Escape from the Ice Palace

Fortunately the courtyard was deserted, so they were able to enter the main building through a small doorway in a round tower, which revealed a flight of steps spiralling upwards.

They seemed to climb for ever, up and up, round and round until Maddie's legs ached and she felt as if she couldn't draw another breath.

And then, eventually, they found themselves at one end of a long, long corridor that stretched before them for as far as they could see. The passage was dimly lit by single lamps at intervals on the thick ice walls that towered above them on either side.

"Come on," said Sebastian. "We have to go on, we have no choice."

They crept on, keeping close to the corridor wall. It was eerily silent in the dim light and it felt strange to Maddie knowing that everything was made of ice. All she really wanted was to find the key to the padlock that bound Phoebe, to release her and to get out of this awful place. How they were going to do that she had no idea, she only hoped Sebastian knew.

She looked up and it seemed that at last the end of the corridor was in sight, but when they got there and turned the corner, to Maddie's dismay it was only to find another corridor in front of them, identical to the one they had just passed through, and every bit as long.

"Oh, Sebastian," she whispered. "What are we going to do?"

"We keep walking," he replied. By now even his air of bravado had slipped somewhat, although his face was still set and determined. "We have to get somewhere sooner or later."

And it was later, much later, after walking for what seemed like miles, that they heard sounds coming from around yet another corner in the corridor. Eagerly they hurried on, rounded the bend, then stopped as they realized they were in a huge gallery that ran around three sides of a vast space.

Crouching down they crept forward and between thick pillars of ice that formed the supports of the gallery, they peered down to the room below.

"It's the throne room!" gasped Maddie.

"And there," breathed Sebastian, "is the Ice Queen!"

She was sitting in splendour on a throne of sparkling turquoise ice. Her sequinned dress of white satin was trimmed with silver fox fur and the rays of her

sun-shaped head-dress were rapier-sharp icicles. Around her neck thousands of snowflakes formed necklaces while shards of ice dangled from her ears, and the rings on each of her fingers, set with ice-chips, glittered like diamonds as they caught the light.

"Look," breathed Maddie. "There's the key on that chain around her waist."

"Yes." Sebastian nodded. "Goodness knows how we get it."

"Will you use the other spell?" asked Maddie, turning her head to look at him.

Sebastian shook his head. "Not yet," he said grimly. "I've got a feeling we may be needing that for something else."

Maddie looked back to the scene below. The Ice Queen was attended by servants, young girls in white dresses and youths in silver tunics who saw to her every need. Some brought food: exotic fruits and other choice delicacies; others brought drink: pale liquids in transparent goblets. Another group played music on unusual-shaped stringed instruments, whilst still others danced for their mistress's entertainment.

"Are they made of ice as well?" whispered Maddie to Sebastian as they hid in the shadows of the gallery.

Sebastian shook his head. "No," he whispered back, "it's only her army that are made of ice – the guards and the soldiers."

"So who are those other people?" Maddie stared down into the vast room.

"Her servants," Sebastian replied. "The ones who Phoebe told us about, the ones whom her soldiers have captured to serve her."

"People who disappeared in the Enchanted Forest, never to be seen again," breathed Maddie.

Sebastian nodded grimly. "Yes," he said. "And make no mistake, Maddie, if anyone sees us she'll have us captured as well."

Maddie shivered and this time it was more from fright than from the cold.

A sudden shout from below made them both look down again. The Ice Queen had risen to her feet and was pointing with a long silver-taloned finger at one of the servants, a young man with a tangle of black curls.

"Oh dear," said Maddie. "Looks like he could be in trouble. I wonder what he's done."

"Whatever it is, I wouldn't like to be in his shoes," muttered Sebastian.

Even as they watched with a mixture of

awe and dread at what they might be about to see, the Ice Queen began to shriek.

"Bring him to me!" she yelled. "Now! This moment!"

Silence fell on the gathering. Music stopped being played, voices were hushed, dancers grew still. All eyes were turned fearfully towards the throne.

The poor unfortunate boy was seized by two of the Ice Soldiers who frogmarched him to their queen.

"How dare you!" she shrieked as he was forced to his knees before her. "How dare you serve me pomegranate. You know I never eat pomegranate. You wretched youth, you could have killed me!"

"I'm . . . I'm sorry, your M-majesty," stammered the boy.

"Silence!" shrieked the Ice Queen. "Did I give you permission to speak?" She turned to some of her servants who were huddled together in a fearful little group. "Did I say he could speak?" she demanded. "You may answer."

"No, Your Majesty," the servants chorused.

"In that case he needs to be taught a lesson."

Maddie watched wide-eyed with horror as the boy began to struggle.

"Take him away," screeched the Ice Queen. "Keep him in chains. Give him no water or cabbage for two days. I will visit him then and I will personally see if he has learnt to respect his Queen."

As she finished speaking she picked up her whip, the one they had seen her use on Phoebe whilst driving her chariot. She flicked it only once with an evil little crack as the Ice Soldiers began to march the boy away, but it was too much for Maddie.

Leaping to her feet she leaned over the gallery. "Leave him alone!" she yelled.

"Maddie!" gasped Sebastian, clutching at her arm. "Maddie, no!"

But it was too late. Every head in the throne room below was turned in their direction. Every pair of eyes was on them, including those of the Ice Queen who drew herself up to her full height. With one hand on her hip, she pointed her whip at them, the light catching its long silver tip.

"Who is that!" Her voice had risen to an even higher pitch.

Ignoring Sebastian's attempts to silence her, Maddie stared down in defiance. "I'm Maddie," she said in a loud voice. "Maddie O'Neill."

"Do you know who I am?" demanded the queen in an incredulous voice.

"Yes," said Maddie. "I know who you are. You're a cruel, selfish, evil old woman."

A huge gasp rose from the throne room, echoed by Sebastian's groan.

"There are two of them!" yelled the queen. "Seize them. Take them to the dungeons! How dare they! They will wish they'd never been born when I've finished with them!"

"Maddie, come on!" Sebastian was on his feet now and was dragging her away from the rail. "Come on, we must get out of here."

"But . . . that boy. . .!" she protested.

"We can't help him by getting caught ourselves. Come *on*!"

Reluctantly she allowed Sebastian to drag her out into the corridor again. It was still cold and eerily silent but as they began to run they became aware of shouts and cries, and of another sound – the distant drumming of feet as the Ice Soldiers began their pursuit.

"Come on," said Sebastian firmly, "this way. There have to be stairs sooner or later." He took Maddie's hand and together they fled.

When at last they did find a flight of steps they almost missed it because it was tucked away in the shadows of a dimly-lit corner. They would have sped by but it was Maddie who spotted it. She stopped and tugged Sebastian back.

"Look." She pointed. "Steps, leading down."

"Well done," said Sebastian and in spite of her fear, Maddie felt a little glow deep inside.

They sped down the steps which curved round and round and were so steep it was like descending the side of a mountain.

At last they reached the ground floor only to find themselves in yet another maze of corridors. Once again they began to run but then, to their dismay, at the far end of the corridor they saw a group of soldiers.

They turned and fled but the soldiers had seen them and amidst shouts of triumph began to chase them.

"Come on, Maddie. Run!" shouted Sebastian.

They ran and ran, only too aware of the sounds of the soldiers behind them, but as they rounded another corner, they were confronted by a second group, no doubt alerted by the cries and shouts of their comrades.

"Oh no!" wailed Maddie. "What now?"

"We're trapped!" said Sebastian grimly. "They're all after us now."

Then, as with cries of triumph the soldiers began to thunder towards them, he lifted his hand so that the light from one of the lamps high on the wall, dim as it was, caught the emerald in his ring. He took a deep breath.

"Oh," gasped Maddie. "The spell. Can you remember it?" she added anxiously.

"I hope so," Sebastian muttered. "But we can't afford to get it wrong, so to be on the safe side, could we say it together?"

"Of course," said Maddie.

And together they began to chant the words of the second spell:

"Zilleriah over Ziskin.
Zanda. Zoska. Zeen.
Zariander of Zillaban
Appear in a Flame of Green!"

Then as the emerald flashed, in a steady, firm voice Sebastian said, "Warm wind from the south, aid our escape from the Ice Palace."

For a moment Maddie and Sebastian stood transfixed, hardly daring to breathe as the soldiers advanced on them down the corridor.

Then it was Maddie who noticed it first. "It's getting warmer," she whispered. "Don't you feel it, Sebastian? A warm, rushing feeling."

He lifted his head and half-closed his eyes.

"What is it?" said Maddie in

amazement. "Where is it coming from?"

"It's what I asked for," Sebastian murmured, a slow smile spreading across his face. "The warm wind from the south."

"Oh," gasped Maddie suddenly, "look at the soldiers. They are falling over."

And indeed they were. The group that had been bearing down on them were now in a struggling, floundering heap on the ground.

"What's that noise?" Maddie's eyes widened.

Drip. Drip. Drip.

"It's a thaw," said Sebastian. "Everything has started to melt. "Come on," he went on urgently. "This is our only chance, we mustn't waste it."

Without waiting to see more of the Ice Soldiers' fate they began to run. They passed the second group at the other end of the corridor but they, like their comrades, were floundering in large pools of water.

By the time Maddie and Sebastian reached the courtyard the palace seemed to be in a state of chaos with servants rushing here and there and confusion amongst the soldiers as the steady thaw went on.

Above all this could be heard the blood-curdling shrieks of the Ice Queen as she stood on the battlements high above them, shaking her fist and threatening revenge as her regime and her palace began to dissolve around her.

"How dare you!" she screeched. "Come back the lot of you! Ungrateful creatures! Miserable wretches! After all I've done for you! Return this instant. If you don't, you'll be sorry! I shall put curses on you all! I shall freeze the marrow in your very bones! Come back, I say!"

"We have to get Phoebe," shouted Sebastian as with a shudder he glanced back at the demented figure of the Ice Queen. By this time her crown was melting and dripping down her face and her hair was hanging about her shoulders like wet rats' tails.

Together they ran across the cobbled yard, wet and even more slippery now from the melted ice.

"But we don't have the key," cried Maddie.

"I think you'll find we won't need it now," Sebastian replied.

And as they entered the stables and ran through to Phoebe's stall they found that the chains and the walls of the stall had all started to melt and that Phoebe was kicking at the door with her strong legs. The weakened door at last gave way and with a great whinny of triumph the unicorn trotted out to join them.

"Oh Phoebe!" cried Maddie. "Well done!"

"We still have to get out of the palace," cried Sebastian urgently. "I don't trust the Ice Queen."

They rushed from the stables, joined by the horses who had been Phoebe's companions. They were only too eager to join her bid for freedom when she told them that their captivity was over.

So great was the panic outside as servants and animals fled from the evil clutches of the Ice Queen, that no one bothered about the little group who dashed through the side gate. They sped across the ground towards the clump of rocks where Zak and Peregrine waited for them.

"It's about time too," squawked Zak flapping his wings. "I was just thinking I'd have to come and sort things out."

"No need for that Zak," said Sebastian loftily. "Absolutely no need at all."

"No," said Maddie. "Sebastian did it. He was wonderful."

"Oh boy!" said Zak gloomily. "I suppose we'll never hear the last of this now."

The reunion between Phoebe and Peregrine was beautiful and, as they licked and nuzzled each other, so touching it made Maddie want to cry, but Sebastian would not let them linger. Pulling on his cloak, he said, "We must get right away from the palace. There's no knowing how long the warm wind will last, just as there's no knowing what trickery the Ice Queen will get up to when she recovers."

"What about all the servants?" asked Maddie anxiously.

"Don't worry, they will all have escaped," said Sebastian. "That evil woman is on her own for the present." He turned to Phoebe who was still licking Peregrine's face. "Our task is not complete, Phoebe," he said, "until we deliver you both safely to the rest of your herd. Do you know where they are?"

Phoebe tossed her head. "The plan was to go to the Rainbow Lands," she said, "but that will have changed after the attack. I don't think they will have gone too far. They'll be hoping that we will be able to join them."

"I know where they are," said Zak smugly. "They've gone to the foothills of the Mountains of Cloud."

"How do you know that?" asked Maddie, filled with admiration for the raven's seemingly endless knowledge.

Zak shrugged his black shoulders. "I just know these things," he said, nonchalantly blowing on his claws.

"A seagull told him when we were hiding behind those rocks," said Peregrine, and Zak scowled.

Sebastian laughed. "Well, seeing that you know these things, Zak," he said, "you can lead the way."

"Climb on to my back," said Phoebe suddenly. "Come on, both of you."

Moments later the flight from the Land of Frost had begun. Maddie, warmly wrapped in Sebastian's cloak and with his arms around her, sat safe on Phoebe's back. Peregrine galloped behind, and Zak glided ahead as he led the way to the unicorn herd in the Mountains of Cloud.

Chapter Ten

The Wish Is Granted

They rode throughout another night and found the herd just as the dawn was breaking. Pearly golden light touched the mountains and revealed the unicorns grazing quietly amongst the meadows of fresh green grasses.

Even as the friends approached through the soft morning mist one unicorn lifted his head, stared at them, then with a loud whinny of pure delight detached himself from the rest of the herd and cantered towards them.

Phoebe paused for a moment in her flight, and beneath them, Maddie and Sebastian felt her shudder of pleasure. "Cornelius," she breathed, before resuming her headlong gallop.

They stayed to witness the meeting of the unicorns, to tell the story of their adventures, then to rest a while, and to eat: fruit, nuts and berries.

A little later, Zak flew over to Maddie and Sebastian who were resting quietly together beneath the branches of a tree.

"Cornelius is going to take us back to Zenith," said Zak. "He says it's the least he can do to show his gratitude."

It was hard saying goodbye to Peregrine

and to Phoebe but it had to be done, even though the little unicorn cried when Maddie kissed him.

"I'll never forget you, Maddie," he said. "Will you be able to come back and see me again one day?"

"Oh, I hope so," she cried. "I do hope so."

And then it was time to go, and watched by the entire herd Maddie and Sebastian mounted Cornelius's back, and with Zak flying alongside, they waved to Peregrine and Phoebe until they were out of sight.

The sun had begun to sink and by the time they reached the Enchanted Forest it was a huge ball of fire in the west. The forest did not seem nearly such a daunting place now when Cornelius thundered along the pathways.

"Oh look!" It was Maddie who first

caught sight of the woodcutter's cottage and as Cornelius briefly skidded to a halt, the door opened and the old man came down the path to the gate accompanied by his wife.

Leaning against Sebastian, Maddie whispered, "Look, your magic worked. She is fit and well now, Sebastian. You lifted the curse of the Ice Queen."

Sebastian didn't reply, he just tightened his grip on Maddie as he leaned forward to speak to the woodcutter.

"You found the herd then," said the old man.

"Oh yes," Sebastian replied, "we found the herd. Peregrine is with his mother. This is his father, Cornelius. He is taking us home. We are pleased to see your wife looking so well."

The old man beamed. "Yes," he said. "It

was truly amazing, she suddenly got better not long after you had left."

"Amazing," said Sebastian.

"And that's not the only strange thing that's been happening in these parts either," the woodcutter went on. "Many of the people in the villages around here had lost their sons and daughters over a period of time, then quite suddenly, a couple of days ago, they all returned. They had been kidnapped by the Ice Soldiers and held captive by the Ice Queen. . ."

"Did they say what had happened?" squawked Zak, who had settled on the gatepost and was watching the woodcutter and his wife with his head on one side.

"Something very strange," the wood-cutter's wife replied. "The Ice Palace and the Ice Soldiers began to melt, so the young people were all able to escape."

"Get away!" said Zak. "You don't say."

"And the Ice Queen?" asked Sebastian. "What happened to her?"

"No one seems to know," said the woodcutter. "She was last seen fleeing from the melting Ice Palace in a rowing boat, but where she has gone is a mystery. She was screeching revenge apparently, and saying she would be back, but she's pretty powerless without her soldiers, so she's no longer a threat in these parts."

"The villagers are holding celebrations tonight for the safe return of their children," said the woodcutter's wife. "Could you all stay?" She looked hopefully from Sebastian to Maddie, then to Zak.

"We would love to," Sebastian said simply, answering for them all, "but we have to get back. And I'm sure Cornelius is longing to return to Phoebe and Peregrine."

They took their leave of the woodcutter and his wife, and Cornelius resumed the gallop which very soon brought them back to the royal castle.

Zenith was waiting for them on the steps of the East Tower, and Thirza was hovering anxiously behind him.

"Zenith looks very stern," whispered Maddie as Sebastian helped her from Cornelius's back.

It was Zak who answered. "He'll be waiting for Sebastian's report," he muttered just loud enough for Maddie to hear. "He'll be wanting a detailed account of all that happened and how Sebastian chose to use the spells."

"I have a meal ready for you," said Thirza suddenly in her high-pitched, bell-like voice. "So hurry yourselves along before it spoils." She turned and bustled away into the tower, leaving Maddie and Sebastian to take their leave of Cornelius who was pawing the ground, anxious to be away.

"Come to the royal mews before you go," said Sebastian. "We'll give you oats and fresh water before your journey."

"Thank you, Cornelius, for bringing us home," said Maddie as they walked beside him into the stable yard.

"Thank *you*," said Cornelius, "for returning my family to me. And don't forget, if ever we unicorns can help you in any way, you only have to ask."

They watched as he enjoyed a feed of hay and oats and drank a full bucket of water, and then he was gone, thundering away again with his neck arched, tail and mane flowing, anxious to join his family once more.

With a little sigh, Maddie turned and was about to make her way back to the East Tower with Sebastian when she stopped and stared, hardly able to believe what she was seeing.

The Princess Lyra had just come out of one of the horses' stalls. But this was a very different Princess Lyra from the one she had seen the last time. This one was dressed not in clothes of fine silk, but in breeches and a shirt, both of which were covered in mud. Her corn-coloured hair was screwed back from her face and was full of wisps of straw. In one hand she carried a pitch-fork and in the other a bucket.

She stopped when she caught sight of Maddie and Sebastian, a look of horror on her face, then she turned and slunk back into the stall, slamming the door behind her.

"Now, what do you suppose all that was about?" asked Sebastian.

"It *was* the princess, wasn't it?" said Maddie incredulously.

"Oh, yes it was, no doubt about that," said Sebastian. "But goodness knows what she was doing."

Together they made their way back to the East Tower and went inside, where they learnt from Zenith the reason for the Princess Lyra's strange behaviour.

"She was in deep trouble when her father the king returned," he said. "He was very angry when he learnt she'd been keeping a unicorn in captivity, and for once, he didn't let her get away with it." He chuckled suddenly. "And I have to say, he made the punishment fit the crime. She has to muck out the stables every day for a whole month."

"Serves her right," squawked Zak from his perch. "Saying she'd have me shot indeed!"

The meal that Thirza had prepared for their homecoming was more like a banquet, but neither of them had very much appetite. Maddie was too tired to eat and Sebastian was apprehensive about his forthcoming interview with Zenith.

Zak was the only one who really did justice to the meal, tearing at the delicacies with his beak and wolfing down fruit and berries.

At last Zenith pushed his plate away and leaned back in his chair. "Right," he said, "let us hear your account of what happened."

Maddie was a little startled. She had expected Zenith to take Sebastian off to the turret room to question him in

private. She threw Sebastian a quick, anxious glance and was reassured to see that he looked quite calm.

"Where would you like me to begin?" he asked.

"I've always thought the beginning is the best place for that," replied Zenith.

"In that case I'd better start with our journey through the Enchanted Forest," said Sebastian.

Zenith remained silent while Sebastian recounted their adventures, and it wasn't until Sebastian had finished that he spoke.

"You have conducted yourself in a most exemplary fashion," he said at last. "You used each of the spells wisely. The first to help another less fortunate soul than yourselves, which was very commendable. The second, to thwart the evilness of that wretched woman, which showed imagination and great resourcefulness. But most important of all you granted the unicorn's wish by returning him to his mother. I am well pleased with you, Sebastian," the WishMaster concluded, "and I will be awarding you one of the points you need to win your Golden Spurs."

"Thank you, WishMaster," Sebastian replied. "But there is one thing I would like to say. I don't think I would have got through if it hadn't been for Maddie . . . for her good memory, for her courage, her kindness to the others, and for the way she stood up to the Ice Queen."

A sudden, muffled squawk from the perch in the corner made them all turn.

"And Zak, of course," Sebastian added hastily. "They both helped tremendously."

Maddie blushed then, looking quickly

at Zenith, she was surprised to see a smile cross his features.

"This calls for more strawberry cordial," cried Thirza, as she began bobbing around the table refilling their goblets. Maddie nodded in contentment and leaned back in her chair as Sebastian returned the emerald ring to Zenith, who then began asking more questions about the fall of the Ice Palace.

In the end she could fight her tiredness no longer and very gradually her eyelids began to close. . .

There was movement, a gentle movement, and the sound of water, as if it were lapping against the side of a boat.

Maddie opened her eyes.

She was nestled deeply amongst the brightly-coloured cushions in the bottom of Sebastian's boat, and when she lifted her head, she found the boat was sliding beneath the willows in the stream at the bottom of her garden.

Sebastian was standing at the front of the boat, but on hearing a movement from Maddie, he turned to look at her. "You're home, Maddie," he said.

"Oh," she said, and felt a stab of disappointment.

"Thank you," said Sebastian, "for all your help."

"I should think so too," squawked Zak.

When Maddie turned her head it was to find the raven perched at the other end of the boat. "Goodness knows where we would have ended up without her," he added, "if it had been left to you, what with that bad memory of yours."

Sebastian jumped out of the boat on to the bank and when Maddie stood up he took her hand to help her ashore.

"Where will you go now?" she asked, aware of a lump in her throat that seemed to be getting alarmingly big.

"Back to Zavania," he said gloomily. "And to Zenith, I suppose."

"What do you mean, you suppose," tutted Zak. "Of course you'll go back to Zenith. He's your master, for goodness sake."

"So you'll go back to the royal castle?" said Maddie. That meant back to the king and queen and to Princess Lyra, she thought miserably.

"Oh, for goodness' sake, you two," snapped Zak. "There will be other times."

"Will there?" asked Maddie hopefully.

"Would you come back another time?" asked Sebastian.

"Oh yes," sighed Maddie. "Of course I will."

"Hadn't you better get indoors?" said Zak, as Sebastian stepped back on to the boat. "Won't your mother be wondering where you are?"

As the boat began to drift away downstream and she sadly waved farewell to Sebastian and Zak, Maddie suddenly felt guilty. She'd forgotten all about her mother in the time she'd been away, and about how her mother had told her not to be long. She frowned. Just how long had she been?

It had been ages! Days even!

She was going to be in terrible trouble, she thought, as with one last lingering look at the V-shaped ripples in the stream, which were all that remained of Sebastian's boat, she began to make her way up the garden to the house.

But somehow, no matter how much trouble and fuss there might be, she had to admit, it had all been worth it, and if she did have the chance to go again, she knew she would do so without any hesitation at all.

She met her mother coming out of the back door.

"Oh, Maddie," she said, "there you are."

She didn't sound cross, not like Maddie would have expected her to be after her daughter had been out for such a long time. She sounded quite normal, in fact, just as she might have done if Maddie had spent half-an-hour playing in the garden.

"I wondered where you were," her
mother went on, "you seemed so upset
when you came home from school. You
really mustn't worry about having to wear
your brace, you know. And as for the
other children, well they'll soon get used
to it, and after a while, they simply won't
take any notice."

Maddie stared at her mother, for the moment wondering what on earth she was talking about. With all that had happened she'd quite forgotten the brace on her teeth. Wonderingly she lifted her hand to her mouth. The brace was still there.

"You'd better come in now, and wash your hands." Her mother turned to go back indoors. "It's nearly time for tea."

Slowly, with her heart thumping, Maddie followed her. It couldn't possibly only be teatime. She had been so far, seen so much, done such incredible things.

If it was only teatime, time must have stood still. What could be the explanation for that?

But then, how could she explain a raven who talked? Or unicorns? Or a whole

army whose soldiers were made of ice?

Maybe it was better not even to try, and then the next time no awkward questions would be asked. Because without any doubt, Maddie knew there would be a next time.

Sebastian would come back for her.

It was just a matter of waiting for someone else to make a wish.

Mermaid Wishes

In the magical land of Zavania, a frightened
mermaid has made a wish. . .

Seraphina is desperately ill, almost dying.
Her beautiful golden hair is tangled and
matted, and without her own enchanted
comb she will never recover. She has
wished for it back. But who took it?
Where is it now?

Sebastian, Maddie and Zak must find the
comb, and grant the mermaid's wish.
And they must find it quickly, for
Seraphina is fading fast. . .

Princess Wishes

*In the magical land of Zavania, a proud
princess has made a wish…*

The spoilt Princess Lyra has made a
wish for her brother to come home –
and insists on accompanying Maddie,
Sebastian and Zak on their mission
to find him.

As the trail leads from a city built on
water to the sinister Mountain of Sun, it
looks like the prince has got mixed up in
something dangerous. Can the friends
overcome their differences in time to
save the day?